Smoke

&

Ember

MOUNTAINS &
MAGNOLIAS
PUBLISHING

SMOKE
& Ember

By Jenny Beth Hall

Scripture quotations taken from The Holy Bible, New International Version®, NIV®. Copyright © 1973, 1978, 1984, 2011 by Biblica, Inc. Used with permission of Zondervan. All rights reserved worldwide.

Printed in the United States of America.

For information address:

Jenny Beth Hall, C/O Mountains & Magnolias Publishing
932 Oldham Dr, Box 384, Nolensville, TN 37135

Published by Mountains & Magnolias Publishing

Edited by Tri-Star Business Dynamics. LLC

ISBN: 979-8-9991894-5-5

First Edition September 2025

DEDICATION

I was only four when I first watched my dad jump out of a plane. To this day I can still see the parachutes bursting open one by one, drifting through the sky like autumn leaves falling from the trees. That image has stayed with me ever since. My father's stories of smoke jumper school, and the countless jumps he made, in and out of service, were always a highlight of my childhood. Likewise, my grandfather's storytelling from his time with the Fire Department in small town Texas also lingers in my memories.

This book is dedicated to the men and women who serve — whether by air, water, fire, or any other line of duty. To those who take it a step further and place themselves directly in harm's way, your courage does not go unnoticed. And to those who love and support them — you are seen, and you are deeply valued.

Love,

JB

Contents

Prologue
7 years ago

EMBER

The tents are up, sleeping bags rolled out, and the Greene Family Ranch crew is gathering around the fire. Some family members are sitting on logs, others in camp chairs, while Tommy and Rex string up hammocks between the trees nearby. The two of them are close as brothers — inseparable since before kindergarten and always underfoot with their wild ideas and nonstop teasing. Our annual post-harvest camping trip is officially underway.

"Alright y'all, gather round," Daddy calls. The deep baritone in his voice travels through the campground like a foghorn calling us to all gather around the fire. When Daddy speaks, everyone listens.

We all settle in. Momma and Grandma take spots to Daddy's left, while Grandpa and Uncle Mike sit to his right. A moment later, my great-aunt and uncle arrive with their son Paul and squeeze in at the end. I find my place between Momma and Grandma.

A couple of our ranch hands, Jeremy and Luis, join the circle with their own plates and quiet laughter. They've worked at the ranch with us for years and are as much part of the family as anyone born into it. Jeremy, tall and quiet with a dry sense of humor, leans over and throws a handful of marshmallows at Rex and Tommy, then mouths something that makes both boys laugh. Luis, who always brings his guitar on these trips, is already tuning it softly, waiting for the perfect moment to play. Ms. Sally, Rex's mom, and our ranch cook claims the final camp chair around the fire, her own plate in hand. Altogether a dozen of us sit around the campfire tonight.

"C'mon, Waylon, get to it so we can eat," my Uncle Mike says with jest toward my dad.

My mom elbows him in fun, then turns to Daddy. "Yes, dear, hurry and say the blessing so we can eat. I'm famished." Momma's always hungry after setting up camp—honestly, I am too.

"Alright, everyone bow your heads," Daddy says. Around the campfire, heads bow and eyes close. "Lord, thank You for this time together as a family. We are grateful for all You've blessed us with this season. We are grateful for the bountiful harvest, the land bestowed upon our family for generations, and our old-fashioned cowboy ways. Thank You for Miss Sally's cooking and prep for this trip and all the meals she prepares for us. Thank You for the family that's come before us and those who will continue after us. Thank You for the friendships that grow through trials and good times. Thank You for this cowboy life. In all glory and honor, we give to You our lives and futures. Amen."

Around the fire voices answer in chorus, "Amen."

Daddy clears his throat and adds, "Let's not forget Psalm 90:2, 'Before the mountains were born or you brought forth the whole world, from everlasting to everlasting you are God.'" He pauses, looking out toward the dark ridge line of the Bitterroots. "Nothing like the mountains to remind us how small we are, and how mighty He is. Let's eat!"

"Dig in!" Miss Sally says as the ranch crew start to crack open the aluminum tents on their plates.

Miss Sally truly does make the best food. She joined the ranch when I was four and has been here for the last ten years. Tonight, she's treating us to bison foil packs, bison meat with potatoes, carrots, and spices she refuses to reveal to anyone. But I think there's some rosemary in there for sure. Her son Rex is my brother Tommy's best friend. They're the same age and are going into their senior year in high school

After a long harvest, this year's camping trip feels extra special. We all needed a few days away. While we are all out here on our camp trip, we will get to float, kayak, and just spend time away from our normal ranch duties. Daddy says it's a great place to forget about the world and spend time with God, so every day we'll also have a morning Bible study in the wild — usually over one of Miss Sally's fantastic camp pancakes and bear sausage. We've been doing this post-harvest trip for as long as I can remember, and it's always something I look forward to.

Before I even get the aluminum tent popped open on my plate, Tommy and Rex are poking fun at me.

"Watch out, Ember's going to high school this year," Tommy says with an exaggerated whisper, like it's some terrifying prophecy.

"Yeah," Rex chimes in, tossing a stick into the fire. "Better watch your back, she's going to get all moody and mysterious now. High school girls get like that."

"Like you two know anything about girls," I shoot back, rolling my eyes as I finally manage to unroll the aluminum and let the steam trapped inside the makeshift tent escape. The aroma hits my senses, and I breathe it in.

Tommy grins. "We know enough to stay out of your way when you get that look in your eye."

"What look?" I ask, raising a brow.

"That one!" they both say in unison, cracking up and dodging away from me as I fork a potato and fling it at them. It gets closest to Tommy, and he dodges it, almost flipping himself over in his hammock. Everyone, including me, laughs. This is what it's always like with them. Easy, fun, and safe.

As I sit back down, I catch Rex glancing my way. His teasing smile is gone, replaced by something quiet as he takes me in. For a second, we just look at each other. It's not a big moment, not one anyone else would notice, but it feels like something. Something small and new and ours. Then he looks away, scratching behind his ear and nudging Tommy with a joke, and just like that, it's gone. But I tuck it away, he's Tommy's best friend and a senior this year. Way out of my league.

As we eat, conversation drifts into stories. Grandma brings up the year the tents flooded, and everyone had to sleep in the horse trailer. Uncle Mike adds something about Rex snoring so loud that year he scared off a black bear. Rex rolls his eyes and laughs, shaking his head as Tommy throws in an exaggerated bear growl.

Daddy leans forward and pulls the old wooden walking stick from where it leaned against his seat. He turns it over in his hands, the firelight flickering across its surface, before he pulls out a pocketknife and carves a new notch.

"Thirty-five notches," he says, running his thumb over the carved lines, some darkened with age. "Started this tradition when I was sixteen with my dad. The only year I missed was the one when your grandma broke her leg and we had to camp inside instead."

"Still made pancakes," Grandma chimes in proudly.

We all smile. That stick is more than just wood now. It holds memories, a timeline of our family.

The mountains around us, tall, rugged, and painted in shades of red and gold, seem to glow in the evening sunset; the stars twinkling out in the sky above the ridge line. The color from the quaking aspens and western larches turning brilliant hues in the fall, their gold and scarlet leaves lighting up the hillsides like fire. The Bitterroot Mountains in autumn are something special. The air is crisp but not yet cold, scented with ponderosa pine and the sweet smoke of our fire. There's a kind of quiet here that settles into your bones and makes you feel like time slowed down, and it is always just enough time to let you catch your breath and reset.

After dinner, we scatter in small clusters. Luis plays a soft melody on his guitar, and Grandma starts humming along. Paul and Jeremy start a game of cards at one of the picnic tables. The rest of us gradually filter toward our tents and sleeping bags, carrying the warmth of the fire with us.

I snuggle into my sleeping bag, my head

resting just under the flap of the tent where I can still see the sky. The stars twinkle through the branches above like diamonds scattered across velvet.

These people, our family, are everything to me. They're loud and kind and messy and imperfectly perfect. And I know I won't always have this. In a few years, I'll be off chasing my dreams, maybe in another state, maybe traveling, living out of a trailer, and helping animals on the road. I want to be a veterinarian, and not just one with a clinic, but one who moves where she's needed. Ranches, rodeos, wildfires, floods. I want to help in the middle of it all.

But I also want this. The feeling of belonging. Of knowing there will always be someone to pull you close when the wind picks up or the night gets too quiet.

"The sky's full of extra stars tonight, I think," my Momma says as she sits next to me. "I'm betting that God's poking extra holes in the sky to let the light shine down just for you."

Above us, the Montana night stretches wide and endless, a blanket of midnight blue speckled with galaxies. Out here, away from the pollution of city lights, the sky is the kind of black that lets every hue shine through. The stars don't just twinkle. Out here they have the room to blaze. Some burn soft yellow, others bright white. A few shimmer in pale blue and deep red, and it's the first time I really notice how colorful they can be when you have the space and stillness to see them right.

"Momma," I lean my shoulder into her, smiling at the old story she used to tell me as a kid, about how God adds stars to the sky by poking holes in the navy blanket He holds up to cover the sun so we can sleep. She would say that God would know when a kid was scared of the dark and poke another hole to let more light shine in. When I was little, I believed it with my whole heart. Now, it just feels silly. "I don't believe that anymore," I say.

"Well, maybe not," she says with a knowing smile. "But it could still be true. Have you ever been able to count the stars all at once?"

She smiles that beautiful, loving smile that I genuinely believe every Momma has. Her blue eyes sparkle like sapphires, and her red hair glows, the color of the flames enhancing the color of her red hair. I'm sure mine looks the same. I got my red hair from her. Ever since I was born it has been deep auburn-red; my hair is why they named me Ember instead of Alice. Momma had always said she wanted a girl named Alice, but when Daddy saw me, he said my hair reminded him of the color of glowing embers.

And as I lay there, wrapped in the hush of the trees and the steady rhythm of crickets, I let myself believe, even if it's just for tonight, that this would last forever. That the stars would always shine this bright, the fire would always crackle nearby, and the voices I love most would always be within reach. The next few days we'll fish, hike, and laugh some more. But for now, I close my eyes beneath the big Montana sky, with my heart full and my dreams waiting just beyond the dawn.

Chapter 1
Starboard Reunion

EMBER

The music in the cruise ship's club is pulsing tonight, like the heartbeat of the ship itself is reverberating through the metal and the high gloss dance floor. It's no different than every other night we have been in this floating city adrift in the ocean, but now that the cruise is half over and there are only two nights left on this ship before we return to port in Miami, it seems that everyone wants to come out to play.

1

The bass is thumping, the bodies are swaying, and over at the bar leaning into a guy who looks old enough to be my dad, is my best friend, Katie. Don't get me wrong, he's good looking for a silver-fox, but not my type. Katie, however, loves an older, more mature man.

Katie is thoughtful and kind, but also trouble in every sense of the word. She's refined, beautiful, and has more of her Daddy's money than anyone should be allowed. She once talked her way into a five-star hotel kitchen in New York City just to try making crème brulé and walked out with a job offer and a marriage proposal. She's tall, with long legs, beautiful black hair that goes right to small of her back, eyes that sparkle like golden topaz, and built with perfect proportions. Men see her, women want to be her, and she is as oblivious as it comes to both.

Then there's me. Ember Greene. Small town Montana ranch girl, and plain as can be. Unlike Katie, I am all too aware of people. And after three nights on board, I am peopled out.

Moving to Durham, North Carolina for college and becoming best friends with my southern debutante roommate, Katie, quickly broadened my horizons for sure. Her family has a large home in the Outer Banks that we have

2

visited often. Her mother, a world-renowned author, traveled constantly and would bring the two of us along for company. I loved the experiences it gave us, but it made me long for something simpler, like small town Montana.

With the start of our senior year of college coming up, Katie had convinced me to come on this cruise for what she called 'well needed downtime.' In Katie's mind that meant time away from our normal routine, and expanding her dating pool. Debutante or not, she enjoyed equal opportunity dating.

Many of the men we have met have been interesting, mostly Europeans checking out our side of the globe. Some of them have been kind and nice enough to talk to, but others have been no less detestable as anywhere else I have been. If nothing else, they have all been fun to talk to. No one I would take home to meet my parents though.

From here I see the silver-fox reach over to Katie and gently push her hair behind her shoulder, before running the tips of his fingers over her bronzed skin, then sliding them down her arm. That gesture means it is now time to make my presence known and rescue her before she gets herself in bigger trouble.

I start making my way across the dance

floor towards Katie, slowly easing through the bodies that are moving and grinding together, excusing myself as I go. I am struggling to get past a pair of young women who are dancing raucously with an overeager young man when an unmistakable voice like honey on warm biscuits stops me dead in my tracks. I haven't heard it in years, but I would know it anywhere.

"Well, look who the sea drug out with the tide."

Rex Madison.

How in the world did I end up on the same cruise ship as him way out in the ocean?

I am surprised but also excited to see him; it's been years since I have hugged his neck. The last time I saw him in person was when he left for the military. Since then, it has been in pictures on social media, or in the stories his mom tells when she came over for breakfast on Saturdays.

When I turn around and see him standing there, I am not let down. I can hardly contain my excitement before I throw myself into his arms for a hug.

"Rex!" I smile big. "Imagine my surprise at seeing *you* here!" I pull away long enough to glance up and notice how much taller, broader, and tanner he seems than the last time I saw him; I was just fifteen then.

"Same, Emie." He hugs me tight then lets me go, backing up just enough to put space between us, but close enough that it allows us to talk over the music that has grown obnoxiously loud.

"Rex, you can't call me Emie anymore," I shake my head playfully and motion with my hands from head to toes, "I grew up."

"Yes ma'am you did." He smirks a grin at me that makes his dimples stand out more. It doesn't hurt that he has obviously been getting sun and has his own nice summer glow radiating from his skin.

Ugh, why does he have to be my brothers best friend?

"So, who you here with?" he asks.

"Katie, my college roommate. She insisted that we needed to do something fun before our last year. She managed to convince me that *this* should be it." I hold my hands out and gesture to the ship around us.

"Not enjoying yourself?" he gives me an inquisitive look.

"It's fine. We have snorkeled, hiked in the Bahamas, swam with the pigs, and done all the things. But," I look back over my shoulder to where Katie is sitting, "as you can tell, she's way more interested in what she's finding on the ship."

Rex leans in over my shoulder to see where I am looking, the closeness of his body makes me go rigid. He smells like coconuts, lime, and memory.

"Well, he doesn't look so bad," Rex says with a light chuckle. "He's just a little weathered, like a sea turtle." He laughs at his own joke.

"Rex!" I laugh, "Did you miss that he looks old enough to be her dad?"

A deep chuckle in his chest creeps out between his beautiful lips, "Okay Em. Just remember, some of us go gray sooner than others. See?" He points to two little gray hairs at his ear, "I found those this morning. I'm twenty-five."

I laugh at him. "You asked me what I am doing here, but what about you?" Curiosity gets the better of me before I can stop myself, "Are you here with a woman?"

"No, ma'am. I just got out of the military. I had an opportunity to getaway and thought that it would be worthwhile while I wait on my next adventure."

Rex was always one for an adventure and *always* getting my brother Tommy in trouble with him. They had scaled up the water tower in our small town and rappelled from the side one year, which got them in trouble with a capital T. Another time, they rearranged the rock M on the side of the hill in our town that stood for Moose Hollow. They worked all night to make it a W instead. Those two were always up to something.

"Adventure? Or trouble?" I give him a lively poke, and he playfully swats away my hand.

"Adventure, Em. I grew up too." Looking at him, I can clearly see that, no questions there. "I am headed to Smoke Jumper school in a few weeks, right there in Missoula. I will get to be close to home for a few months."

"You're going back to Montana?" A pang of longing I haven't felt before hits me, but I still don't know if I will ever go back other than to visit.

"Yes. At least for now. I can go anywhere

in the country after school is over, and I already have fire departments that are recruiting me. With my smoke jumper training, I will likely end up somewhere on the western side of the country."

"Wow. That's really cool, Rex." I take a sip of my umbrella drink, it tastes like coconut and pineapple, and there's a gummy shaped shark floating in it. Maybe I haven't grown up after all.

"Yeah," Rex says as he runs his fingers through his hair and smiles at me, "since I will only be an hour away, if I get some downtime, maybe we can get together and hangout. Perhaps I can even take you to dinner sometime?"

Did Rex Madison just ask me out? No way, this is not happening. Tommy would kill me, but the 15-year-old girl inside me is squealing right now.

I smile at Rex, but I am going to have to let him down, carefully of course. "Rex, that's so sweet, but I am still in college this year. Katie and I are going back to North Carolina after the cruise. We have two weeks 'til school starts and need to unpack our storage unit from the summer."

If I didn't know better, I would say big and tall, muscle bound, tough guy Rex, looks like someone just blew out the candles on his birthday cake. He recovers quickly, then he smiles at me, "Alright then. How about tomorrow for lunch? Me and you, lunch on the upper deck? My treat. You can even bring Katie if you want."

"Is that a bribe to get me there? And what will Tommy think?" I give Rex a smile that is part curiosity and part enthusiasm.

"Tommy will think it was downright noble that I stumbled across his baby sister in international waters and made it my duty to look after her and made sure to take care of her health and well-being."

His choice of words strikes me as amusing, and I laugh out loud. "Health and well-being it is then. What time is lunch?"

"Meet me at the main staircase at eleven?" I don't think he has stopped smiling since we started talking. That smile is sweet, but it also gives me a tingle I shouldn't have. I think about it a moment longer before letting the 15-year-old girl have her way, "See you at eleven, Rex."

Rex's dimples deepen as his smile

widens. His hand comes up to my shoulder and he squeezes a gentle goodbye. "You should go check on your friend." He nods his blonde head in Katie's direction.

As I turn back to Katie, she's walking away from the bar with the silver fox. That's not good. I turn back to thank Rex, but he's gone. Nowhere in sight.

Katie is headed to the starboard side of the ship and they're about to go in the door to where the staterooms are.

"Katie!" I shout to get her attention, but she doesn't seem to hear me right away. "Katie! Wait up!"

As the silver-fox pushes the door open for them, she turns back to look at me and motions to the man that she needs a moment before coming toward me.

"Yes ma'am?" Katie asks quietly.

"Where are you going? Who's that?"

"He's a nice man; we are just going into the AC to cool off a bit and get out of the humidity."

"Alone?" I question her because that's not like my overly friendly, yet guarded, friend to do.

"Yes, I am so hot," she fans her face which is noticeably pale.

"Okay, but maybe stay somewhere public, don't go behind closed doors."

She smiles at me then, "Why Ember Lynn Greene, what kind of floozy do you take me for?" Katie's southern twang just quadrupled as she feigns offense, then a delicate smile spread across her face. I cock my head at her and give her the look that says *We have been college roommates for three years* but before I can say it out loud, Katie kisses me on the cheek and winks as she walks away, "I'll be back soon."

"Wait! Want to join me and a friend for lunch at eleven tomorrow? I ran into someone from back home."

"No honey, you go on." With that, Katie tosses her black hair over her shoulder and steps through the door with silver-fox-up-to-no-good.

Standing there on the starboard side of the ship, I am awe struck to think that out here in the middle of the big blue ocean I ran into Rex Madison, and we are going to lunch tomorrow. As ready as I am to get my land legs back, I am looking forward to what tomorrow brings.

There was always something special about Rex. Him, my brother Tommy, and I were all close as kids, hanging out at the ranch while his mom cooked, and the three of us played together after chores were finished. That changed when the boys went to high school and left me behind, at least for a while.

I always found myself stealing glances at Rex. Now I can't help but wonder if somewhere along the way, he might have felt the same.

Chapter 2
Prayers on the Upper Deck

EMBER

"Yellow or pink?" I say again for the third time to Katie.

Katie laughs at me as she stands up from where she was sitting on the bed in our cabin and heads over to me, "Sugar, you can't wear pink with that red hair of yours; that's a hard no," she says as she throws the pink one on the bed over her shoulder, "But this yellow one? It's creamy like butter and sunshine. This one will

13

make you stand out in a crowd. Especially with that beautiful summer tan you have going on. I am going to make you a southern lady yet." She holds the dress up in front of me while peeking over my shoulder, smiling like she knows something I don't.

I laugh at her, "If you haven't changed me into one of those southern belle's yet, I am not sure you ever will."

"I still have time to work on you, honey." She leans in and kisses me on the cheek before she retrieves a pair of shoes from her bag, one of seven that she packed for a five-day cruise, and tosses them at me. They're little white kitten heels with three straps across the toes. "Those will compliment those long legs of yours and make him drool."

"It's not a date, Katie!" I say, trying to tell myself that more than her.

"Really? Cause I am pretty sure I have seen you prepare for a *date* with less care in the world than I have seen you parade around this cabin preparing for lunch with *Mr. Rex Madison*, the cowboy-military-firefighter-man that you have not stopped talking about since you saw him last night." She puts her hands on her hips and gives me that look that says, try again.

I shrug. I can't say that I haven't hoped in my mind that it's a date. I might have even prayed about it this morning while I was talking to Jesus. It was more for Tommy to not hurt Rex if something were to come out of it, but it was still prayer.

I slide the yellow dress over my head and pull it into place before slipping into the kitten heels and brushing my hair one last time. I look in the mirror and Katie's right, because of course she is, the yellow dress highlights my tan, and the heels show off my legs.

"How do I look?" I ask one last time before I head out to meet Rex. Butterflies in my stomach and stars in my eyes, even if I am not willing to admit that out loud.

"Divine! He won't be able to resist!" she clasps her hands and smiles at me.

My cheeks get warm, and I am sure that if I were to look at my reflection I would see that my face is as red as my hair. She does know how to make a girl feel good.

"Thanks, Katie." I hug her then head down the hallway to meet Rex at the stairwell.

On my way there I pop open my cell phone and turn the airplane mode off long enough to jump on the Wi-Fi and check my email. A message from the university about class start dates, a message about an internship at a vet hospital, and one from momma that she sent two days ago.

Subject: We Miss You!

Hi Babygirl!

Hope you and Katie-bug are enjoying your trip! We got a late summer calf, she's precious. Your brother named her Meathead, I said absolutely not. When you get off the ship we can video chat and you help us come up with a name.

It feels like you have been gone ages, but I know you were just here a few weeks ago. Since then, we have had lots of storms, and more lightning then I ever remember seeing in the thirty years I have been on the ranch. But the rain has been good for the lowlands. The Chinook Winds are blowing early this year and it's drying out the high land sooner than normal.

16

Weather man says we are still in a drought, but sometimes it's hard to tell that when I see the crops coming in.

How's Katie? Is she still trying to doll you up every chance she gets? Haven't you told her that she can take the girl out of Montana, but she can't take Montana out of the girl?

Daddy and grandma say hi! We love you! Enjoy the trip!

Love, Momma
XOXOXO

I smile at the email; they are always supportive of what I do and keep me updated with what's going on at home. I shut down the Wi-Fi but plan to respond after lunch; I am about to meet Rex momentarily. I am sure he will want me to tell them hi and I am sure I will have more to tell them then. Miss Sally, his mom, retired last year so they don't get updates about him as often, but I do know he calls sometimes just to say hello. After all, our family was like his growing up.

As I come around the corner Rex is casually leaning against the wall like he's been waiting on me for hours and not minutes. He's even more handsome than when we were kids, and that linen shirt being buttoned down a few extra buttons shows off his physique.

Wow. I am having lunch with Rex Madison.

REX

If I thought that Ember was pretty in high school, then she's a full-blown heart stopper now. She's a simple woman but her natural beauty is stunning. When the sunlight hits her hair, it looks like it's glowing, and that yellow dress she has on shows off her tan. These last few years in the south have done her well, but there is something about the woman before me that is still the girl I remember.

Keep your head on Rex, I tell myself. She's a gorgeous woman, but she's also my best friends little sister. I shake it off quickly and keep my smile poised in her direction.

"You look like a ray of sunshine." I say warmly to Ember as I reach out to hug her.

"Thank you," her cheeks are a little pink. Not sure if its blushing or the sun she's been

18

getting on the ship. "Are we ready?"

"Yes Ma'am." *Am I ever!* I put my arm out for her, and she easily slips her hand into the crook of my arm.

We headed up toward the upper deck, moving slowly. There was island music playing somewhere nearby; the sound of the steel drums gently wafting around the ship from a live band.

The top deck opened wide, sunlight bouncing hard off the ocean, blinding and brilliant. I led the two of us toward a quieter spot off to the side, under one of the canvas awnings. A table near the railing with a beautiful view and less noise, which hopefully also meant less distractions. She didn't question it, just walked by my side and let me pull out a chair for her.

"Still the gentleman, huh?" Ember teased me, a smile tugging her lips as she watched me take my own seat.

I shrugged and grinned, settling across from her. "Some things stick. Your dad did an excellent job of teaching me what a man should be for a woman."

She smiles at that, "Yeah, he's always

been good to Momma, and every other person he has ever met."

Just as our food arrived, grilled fish and lemon rice for me, and something veggie-packed and beautiful for her, I glanced up and asked, "Mind if I pray for us?"

Ember looked surprised for half a second, then her expression softened completely. "I'd really like that."

So, I bowed my head, "Lord, thank You for this meal, for old friends and unexpected reunions. Thank You for safety, for second chances, and for whatever comes next. Amen."

As I looked up I noticed a kind smile on her face. It wasn't the polite kind of smile people wear when they're tolerating faith, it was something warmer. Her Dad was the one who had led me on my faith walk until I left the ranch and I was grateful that it had stuck with me. Seeing Ember's face, I think she is too.

We started out slowly: where we'd been, what we'd done. I told her about the years I had been away, the military, the war, and the invite to smoke jumper school when I was transitioning out of the service. She told me about college, the long hours, the late nights at clinics, the dream of Veterinarian school that hadn't let go of her since she was twelve. But somewhere between my third bite of grilled fish and her second sip of lemonade, it stopped feeling like catching up.

We weren't stealing glances across a campfire, or across the room anymore. This started feeling like coming home, like we had just been away from each other for hours, and not years. Like lunch was always on our calendar, and conversation was about our day.

She laughed at my story about the time I landed on her brothers doorstep in college to raise heck with a blowhorn and megaphone, only to show up during quiet hours of finals week. Her laughter was genuine and real, and it sounded like a melody; I had missed that sound.

"I swear, Rex," she said, wiping her eye, "you might just be trouble after all."

"I make memories, sometimes they're… messy."

Ember leaned in then, elbows on the table, her hands folded under her chin, her tone softer. "Yeah. That sounds about right."

I studied her for a second. The way the wind danced in her hair. The way the sun brought out freckles like little stars dancing on her cheeks. The way her blue topaz eyes sparkled and danced when she laughed. Ember was all grown up, and staring at her, I knew I would take extra care of her heart, if she let me. And something about that settled deep in my chest, like recognition and a tinge of regret all wrapped up together.

"You always wanted to be a vet," I said. "Even back then. You would find every injured creature you could and do your best to help and save them."

She laughed again, but it faded slower this time. "And you always helped me find a shoe box and dig their little graves when it didn't work."

I nodded, my gaze steady, "You always felt everything a little more than the rest of us."

A long peace-filled silence stretched between us, filled with waves slapping softly against the hull and the distant hum of music. I leaned forward, voice low.

"Can I ask you something?" he said. "Do you feel a little tug, too? Maybe then, maybe now?"

Ember's lips parted, her eyes narrowing like she wasn't sure if she wanted to answer, but then she did.

EMBER

"Yes," I answered him quietly. "I felt it. I just didn't know what to do with it. You were older and leaving soon for the military, and I was Tommys little sister, and that meant you were off limits." I watched the words land. They hit him softer than I expected, but deeper. "Now? Now I don't think I can help but feel it."

He looked down at the table, then back at me. "I thought about telling you before I left. I wrote it all down once. Even practiced. But you had plans, and I didn't want to stand in the way of that." Rex looks at me with soft eyes. He reaches across and touches my hand.

"You wouldn't have. I would have figured it out, but... Tommy might have had something to say." I look up at him and there's a half smile on his face, "If I am being honest, Rex, I was always waiting for you to come home for a visit, but you never did; we just got pictures and stories from your mom."

The way he looked at me then, quiet, still, full of the things we never said, it made my chest ache. "I did come home, but it always seemed to be when you were at a camp, or a rodeo, or that time you and your mom went to

Texas for her family reunion. I always hoped to see you."

"What about now?" I ask, holding my breath, hardly able to believe that I asked him such a bold question.

His fingers glide from the top of my hand, to brush against mine, not quite holding, but not letting go either. "Now I'm wondering what happens next."

My breath caught. There it was. The moment.

Before either of us could say anything else, a gust of warm ocean air blew napkins across the table and in my attempt to catch them I knocked over a glass of water, spilling it in his direction. He jumped up, laughed, and reached for other napkins to wipe up the liquid, as he did, he knocked over his own glass, straight in my direction. I jumped up and laughed too. Half startled, half relieved.

I looked at him and smiled. "See? Trouble."

Rex smile lingered back at me as the two of us stood there, still as statues. The warm ocean wind blowing over the deck of the ship carrying the sound of the music playing in the distance. But that rapid beating that felt like wild horses galloping across the valley that was reverberating in my chest? That was all Rex.

He stepped toward me, brushed my hair behind my ear, and his gaze held soft and steady on me. My voice was a whisper, but it carried a simple truth with it. "This time... I won't mind the trouble so much."

Like a kernel of truth was just set before us, we were quiet again, but this time it felt like the beginning of something. Like a spark found oxygen and roared into a flame.

And when he reached for my hand, I didn't let go.

Chapter 3
It Felt Like a Dream

REX

Right then, I wanted to kiss her. The way she looked at me, the way it felt like we were supposed to be right here together by design. But I didn't. I knew that I wanted everything with Ember to be perfect, not rushed.

Instead, I took her by the hand, and we walked along the promenade. Off the port side of the ship, small islands passed in the distance.

At one point a pod of dolphins played in the waves nearby. Ember lit up when she saw them, and while she watched the dolphins, I watched her.

When we needed to cool off we stepped inside one of the small restaurants. I helped Ember to a seat then went to order water and ice cream. Strawberry is her favorite; it has been as long as I can remember. When I returned to the table the look on her face told me all I needed to know.

"You remembered!" she said as I set the strawberry sundae in front of her. She wraps her hands around the small dish then looked up at me, the look of joy on her face radiated through her blue eyes.

"It isn't dolphins but based upon the smile on your face right now, I would say ice cream is a close second." I sat down next to her with my own ice cream, vanilla, caramel, pecans, chocolate chips, and a handful of broken salted chips.

"What is that science project?" Ember asked with a look of curiosity and mild disgust on her face.

"A snacky-snack," I smiled back. "One of the guys I was stationed with in Iraq used to conjure up flavors in the dining hall when supplies would get low. This was always the perfect blend of sweet and salty."

"And they happened to have it on this ship?" Now her look is pure curiosity.

"Not a chance. I paid extra to crinkle a bag of chips and pour it on top." I smile at her as I take a big bite. The taste is perfect, and even better without the sand of the desert.

"I will keep to my plain as me strawberry ice cream."

There's a grin on my face as I watch her. "Ember, I don't think you are as plain as you think you are."

"You don't think so?" she says as she takes a bite of her ice cream, and melts into the spoon. "This is so good. Why have I not found this place before today?"

"I don't think so. Not a lot of girls or

women I know that can say they have caught fish with their bare hands, skinned a moose, or fought a porcupine with a trash can lid."

"That porcupine had it coming! He kept me up all night making noises outside my window." She is pointing her spoon at me like this is an inquiry of some kind.

I laugh, then go back to my science project.

Being here with Ember is perfect.

EMBER

After ice cream we went back to walk along the promenade some more; I didn't stop smiling the entire time.

The breeze tugged at my dress, the Caribbean sun warmed my skin, and Rex strolled next to me; my hand in the crook of his left arm again and my shoes dangling in his right. When my feet had started hurting he offered to take me back to my room, but I didn't want to walk away from this, not even for a moment.

For hours we wandered without a plan, making long walks around the promenade, lost in conversation with each other. The laughter of other passengers floated by, but we barely noticed them.

For all we knew, it was just Rex and I on the ship. But for me, everything focused on the sweet stroll, living in the moment.

"Still not tired of looking out at the ocean yet?" I asked, teasing.

"I'm really more of a mountain guy, you know that. But right now? This view's not bad." I look over and expect to see him looking out at the ocean, but he's not. Rex is looking at me, and the butterflies in my stomach erupt into flight. Rex has always been special, but right now, the seeds of feelings I have always had for Rex are blossoming into something more.

We made our way to the back deck where swings stood side by side and people sat watching the ocean fade in the distance. The two of us sat beside each other, just listening to the hum of the ship and watching the wake from the ships engines roll away in waves into the vast blue ocean behind us.

We chatted more about everything and nothing. Eventually Rex checked his watch. "I should let you go; I am sure you have other things to do then hang out with some boy from back home."

I didn't want him to leave, but I nodded. "Um, yeah, I…"

"Meet for dinner?" He spoke so quickly that I couldn't help but smile back at him.

"Yes!" I responded just as fast, a smile on my face.

He smiled. "It's six now. How about eight? Or nine? Meet back at the staircase again?"

"Eight. Don't be late, Rex. I would hate to tell Tommy that you let me down." I smiled suspiciously at him, and he laughed a deep but sweet laugh

"I wouldn't dream of it, Em."

He stood first and helped me up, again with those old ranch manners, and then he walked me back to the hallway that lead to my room. As we parted ways, I glanced back over my shoulder to see him still standing there, a smile on his face, and a warmth that I think meant he also wanted to be more than friends.

Back in my cabin, I stood on the balcony

for a long time thinking about the day. About the conversations Rex and I had. About the feelings we both mentioned we had for each other. Standing there I couldn't help but wonder if God somehow managed to bring us back together for more than just a little lunch date on a cruise.

I say a quiet prayer then connect my phone to the Wi-Fi before climbing onto the bed. I leaned against the headboard and typed out an email back to my mom.

Subject: You'll Never Guess

Hey Momma, (and Dad cause I know you are reading too),

You're not going to believe who I ran into on this cruise.

Rex. Madison.

I know. Of all the people on all the ship's in all the world, I ran into the guy who used to chase me around the barn with chickens and who once punched a hole in a hay bale because I told him he'd never grow taller than Tommy (which of course he did).

He's a smoke jumper now or going to be one soon. A real-life fire-fighting cowboy. And yes, he's still the sweet Rex that he has always been. Thoughtful. Steady. Funny in a way that I'd forgotten. We had lunch together today and we're meeting for dinner tonight. He says hello, by the way.

I'll send pictures when we get to shore. Love you all.

-Ember
XOXOXO

About the time I hit send, Katie bursts into the room, flopping onto her bed in a dramatic sprawl.

"Oh good, you're here! Tell me you have stories, sugar?" her drawl creeping into every word tonight.

I set my phone down as a smile spread across my face, I couldn't hide my excitement if I tried. "I might."

Her eyes get big like the town gossip just landed the biggest story of the entire year. "I presume that things went well with tall, blonde, broad shoulders, eyes like a thunderstorm, Rex?"

I blushed. "We had lunch, we walked the promenade, and we laughed. It was... amazing," I fall back into the bed, like it's a cloud and I don't want to wake from this daydream. "It was like we didn't miss a beat in the last few years, yet it was so completely new. And he is still a Godly man, Katie. It all felt real. Grounded." I dream for a minute of what could be between Rex and I, then take a deep breath and exhale, "And my dad would approve; he taught Rex so much of what he knows."

Katie is staring at me, watching me, with a smile that says she's excited for me. "You're glowing, honey. I have never seen you look like that before."

I laughed, sweeping my hair to the side as I roll over to look at her. "I think I'm just surprised. I didn't expect to run into anyone I know, let alone Rex. There's something there, and I think there always was."

She shrieks with excitement. "Looks like the sun's not the only thing getting warm out here."

"It's not like that," I squeal as I throw a pillow at her, which she catches.

"Mm-hmm. Ember Lynn, I see your face radiating, and I see something new in you. Maybe I need to meet this Mr. Rex and give him my seal of approval."

I smiled again, wide, and unfiltered. "We are going to dinner tonight at eight. Let's see what happens."

She squeals again with excitement and jumps onto my bed with me. "I told you that yellow dress would serve you well!"

Laying there next to my best friend, recounting the afternoon, and dreaming about the future, I feel like this moment is special.

This thing with Rex is going to be something worth holding onto.

Chapter 4
It Happened on a Ship

EMBER

Katie's excitement spilled over into playing dress up for dinner, with me as her living doll. She selected a flowy floor-length black dress that was modest in front, with a low cut back. After I had slipped into the dress, she handed me a pair of red strappy shoes with a four-inch heel.

I lifted the shoes in front of my face and took them in, before holding them out at arm's length toward Katie. The corner of my lip curled up and I opened my mouth using my best Texas drawl to say, "Ya know Katie, my Momma would say, 'There are only two types of ladies who wear heels like that, and you my dear are neither of the two.'" I then drop the heels onto the edge of the bed and Katie bursts into giggles.

She has heard me say that many times before, always mimicking my mommas accent, but today it sounded much more devious. Over the years my momma had been in Montana, her accent had faded, but it had never completely gone away. But that statement was something she used whenever she didn't like anything: bright red nail polish, leopard print anything, or tall heels that represented the lifestyle of the ladies of the night. Now, I said it all the time, more in jest than anything; something about it always made me smile.

I reach into the closet, pick up my sandals, and slide them on instead, "No one is going to see my shoes in this dress."

Katie shrugs and then hands me a pair of abalone earrings, shiny and the perfect accessory for the cruise.

When I am dressed to Katie's specifications for a dinner date with a man I have been pining over for longer than I should admit, she kisses me on the cheek, wishes me good luck, and sends me down the hall for the second time today.

As I walk along, I think about how we got here. The memories from our childhood flood my mind, and I am excited to see how tonight goes, and what memories we might add now.

It's 8pm on the dot and I don't see Rex anywhere. I am starting to think he meant a different staircase, but of course he didn't, because this is the one that we met at earlier today. I am sure if he is late there is a valid reason. I have never known Rex to be late a day in his life.

REX

I was excited, more excited than I should've been for dinner on a cruise ship. But this wasn't just any dinner. This was dinner with Ember Greene. The moment I spotted her across the dance floor, it was like time rewound and gave me a second chance.

The college years had been good for her; she had matured and was even more beautiful than I remembered. The last time I saw her she was all knees and elbows, but now, she had grown into her body, and she was gorgeous. I was proud of myself for asking her to accompany me to lunch, and soon dinner. Nervous, too, but it's in a good way. I want to do right by her, and if Tommy and her dad have anything to say about it, they would expect nothing less.

Even if things went perfectly tonight, after the cruise the two of us might not get a chance to see each other for a while. She would head back to North Carolina, and soon I would head off to Montana for Smoke Jumper school. After school though, I could go just about anywhere.

Of course, I was going to have to figure out how to tell Tommy at some point, but that wasn't my priority right now. Right now, I just wanted to spend time with Ember.

But before that, I had a Bible study to complete. I had been doing a study on men of the bible and was currently in Job. Job is a difficult read, and the first three times I attempted it I struggled, but then it clicked for me one day, and now I read Job with a desire to know more about his heart, and God's heart for him.

Job worshipped at his lowest point; worship was what he turned to despite his circumstances. I wanted to write that in my heart to remember for myself if I was ever challenged.

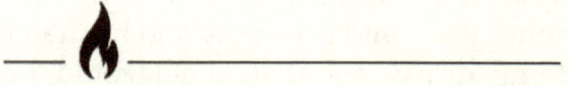

After completing my study, I prayed for a while. I thanked God for all my daily things, food, work, home, life, and asked that he use me in the life of others in a way that brings glory to Him. Today I also prayed a prayer of thanks for Ember and prayed over any future we might have together. Regardless of our future, I prayed for her future.

I cleaned up, shaved, and put on a shirt that didn't look like it belonged in a deployment duffle bag, a white linen shirt I had picked up in one of the stores on board. I showed up twenty minutes early to the staircase meeting point and paced like the floor was hot.

Then my phone rang unexpectedly, a 406-area code- Montana. I ignored it, I have a date with Ember.

The phone rang again, the same number, then another call from my mom. I hesitated for a moment, but I took Mom's call; she knew where I was and wouldn't call me if it wasn't important.

"Hey, Mom."

"Rex," she's sniffling, her allergies must be bothering her. "Are you still on that cruise?"

"Yes ma'am. You would never believe it, but I ran into Ember Greene on the ship. We are heading to dinner together in a few moments."

Silence on the other end, which is strange since Ember is like a niece to her. "Ember's there?" She sounds surprised.

"Yeah. I should see her any minute now."

"Rex…" her sniffles turn into sobbing, "You're sure it's our Ember Greene? You aren't messing with me?"

"Yes, Mom. I spent the whole afternoon with her. Are you okay?" I ask. She's been alone at home since she retired. It's just five acres and close to town, but it's still alone and I have never heard her sound like this. Ever.

"I am fine, I am fine," her voice drops off as she cries some more.

"Mom, you don't sound fine. What's going on?" My other line beeps in again, this time there's a contact affiliated with the number, Chief Warren with the Moose Hollow

Fire Department. I ignore it for now while I talk to mom. A message beeps in; I look at my watch:

Chief Warren: *Hey Rex. Call me asap. I need a favor.*

"Chief Warren reached out to me to see if I had a contact for the Greene Family and I told them I didn't. They were hoping you might since Tommy ... is your best friend," her sobbing continues.

"Mom, I don't know what's going on, but I just got a message from Chief Warren. Let me call him and I will call you back. You're sure that you are okay?"

"Yes. Call him," she says it so softly, like when a movie fades to black.

"Ok, Mom. I love you."

"Love you, Rexy."

I hear her start to cry again before the line disconnects and I dial Chief Warren.

"Rex?" His strong voice echo's through the phone when he answers.

"Yes sir, how can I help you?" I ask.

"You talk to your momma?" His voice is softer now.

"She just called crying, but I didn't get any other than you are looking for a contact for the Greene family. What's going on?"

"I am sorry to bring you into this, but we are looking for next of kin for the family. Do you know who that might be?"

I startle. If they're looking for next of kin, this isn't just serious, it's potentially deadly.

"Sir, everyone lives on the ranch but Ember and a great aunt. I don't know anything about the aunt, but I know where Ember is."

"She's not here in Montana for the summer?" he asks as if he is surprised.

"No sir. She's on a cruise ship. I just happened to run into her last night, and I am meeting her for dinner shortly."

He lets out a long ragged breathe and whispers, "Thank God."

"Chief, what's going on?" I am starting to really worry. Between my mom and stoic Chief Warren, something is going on back home.

"Rex, you know the protocol. I can't tell you without her permission. So, Ember is **not** with you right now?"

"No sir, we are meeting for dinner in about ten minutes or so. Why?"

"I need you to have her call me, and Rex, I am glad you are there. She's going to need a friend. It's bad news."

"Sir?"

"That's all I can say for now, Rex. Call me as soon as she's with you. We will walk through this together."

"Yes Chief, I will do that." Concern hits me as I hang up. He might not be able to tell me, but news travels fast in a small town, and even faster on social media.

I open the social app on my phone, and I don't have to scroll but a few posts down and to see the first hint at what's going on back home. My friend Jack has shared a post from our small county newspaper. The image of a raging wildfire taken from the main street of Moose Hollow, and the camera is staring right at the range that runs through the Greene Family Ranch. Under the picture the headline reads:

"Major Lightning Storm Causes Deadly Wildfire. Department of Natural Resource Says It Spread Quickly. Over a dozen are still unaccounted for."

Below the post the comments are

pouring in with people offering to volunteer to dig fire lines, to help with search and rescue, offering prayers, and hot meals for those working. One comment drops the world out from under me: *I heard there are no survivors.*

The words are just black and white, but they echoed through my whole body. *God, no. Please, not the Greene's.* I closed my eyes and tried to breathe, trying not to panic before we have facts.

I hit my knees right there, before the sounds of the ship blurred into white noise. I couldn't catch my breath; I had to get fresh air.

Lord, I don't know what you're doing here, but I need You. Help me be strong for her, for whatever is coming. Help me not fall apart before we make this call. Help me and Ember to lean into you, Lord.

I stumbled along the promenade, but couldn't process the sound of my mom's tears, the emotions behind Chief Warren's words, and the posts I just saw online. I grab the railing and peer across the horizon as the sunsets in the distance.

All the Greene family's faces are playing on a reel in my mind. All my childhood memories and our camping trips. Then today played back: Em's smile from earlier, her laugh, the way she called me out like she always had. And all I could come up with was a question: *Lord, how am I supposed to tell her?*

I quickly glance at my watch, it's 8:10. I'm late. I'm running back down the stairs, and there she is. Waiting. Looking for me. Smiling. My chest tightens, breath hitching like I've just sprinted through fire.

Lord, help me.

Chapter 5
The Call

EMBER

I glance at my watch one more time, it's 8:05. It's not like Rex to be late, ever. His entire life he grew up in our house, hanging around the ranch, and he was always punctual. He once said that 'on time was late, and late was on time.' Funny enough, my college professor says that now too, I chuckle as I think about the way my professor glared over his glasses as I snuck into class one morning after being late and he made that message a point in his lecture no less than five times that day.

Five more minutes pass anxiously, and I am done waiting. I had allowed myself to get really excited. Just a little flutter, a maybe-he-really-wants-to-see-me-again sort of hope. But instead I would get to put *stood-up-by-my-brother's-best-friend* in the free space on my bingo card on this cruise.

I turn to head to the promenade when I see Rex running down the staircase toward me, and the look on his face tells me that something is wrong.

"Rex?" I walked quickly toward him, "What is it?" When he stops in front of me I notice that his breathing is labored, like he's struggling.

"Ember, let's go to one of our rooms. Yours or mine?" He asks almost wildly.

"Rex, you know that I am not that kind of girl." Concern radiating on his face or not, I am not putting myself in a compromising situation.

"I know you're not, Em." He runs his hands up and down the tops of my arms like he's soothing me, but it disturbs me instead; something is not right. He looks me straight in the eye then, "Listen, I got a call from home, and they asked us to call back together."

Rex's eyes are locked into mine. I don't like this. "Okay, Rex. Let's go back to my room. Katie is still probably there too."

"That's good," he says before he laces his fingers through mine, and we start walking.

The hall is mostly quiet, other than the occasional passerby headed somewhere on the ship. Rex is quiet, and he looks nervous. Thankfully, it doesn't take us long to get to the room.

When I open the door Katie is surprised to see Rex and me. "Katie, this is Rex. Rex this is my best friend Katie."

Katie speaks first, "Rex it's nice to meet you, but I do say you don't look well. Are you okay?"

"Yes ma'am. Nice to meet you. We just need to make a call together somewhere more private than the ships meeting spaces."

"Oh, okay, I can get my things and get out. I was leaving anyway." Katie says as she reaches for her bag.

"No, please stay, Katie. If you're her best

friend, you should be here." He says it in a way that makes my stomach knot. I feel like whatever this call is, it's not good.

Katie's face reflects what I feel as her normal sunshine demeanor seems to fade quickly. "Oh-kay," is all she says as she sets her things down.

"Em," Rex looks at me then, there are tears in his eyes, "before we make this call, know that I am here for you. They wouldn't talk to me, but they said it was important. I am here. Katie is here. We are going to do this together."

I stand there for a moment taking in Rex. He's still tall and handsome, but there is something there now that I can't read. Katie is now sitting on the edge of the bed next to the small couch, I offer her a tentative smile.

"Okay, we do this together."

Rex motions for me to sit on the couch, so I do. He sits next to me, his phone in hand as he dials a name I know: Chief Warren.

"Rex? Is Ember with you now?" Chief's voice sounds less stoic than normal.

"Yes sir. She's right here next to me."

"Ember Lynn? Hi honey, are you okay?"

"Yes sir, why wouldn't I be?"

He takes a deep breath and lets it out slowly, "Ember, there's been a fire..." I look over at Rex and he's staring at me, his eyes full of tears, but he squeezes my hand. "All attempts were made to get to your family, but the wildfire ran down the mountain too fast. I am sorry, Ember, but they're gone."

Katie gasps from across the room. Rex's tears have broken free and are starting to roll down his face.

"Surely you're wrong, Chief. Daddy took great care to always be ready."

"I know, Em. I know he did, but this fire and the wind, it's out of control."

Silence settles into the room, the phone radiating just the noise of Chief Warren's breathing before he starts to speak again, and I hear a quiver in his voice. "Ember I am sorry, but there are no survivors at the ranch."

"Which ranch? Wait, what?" My mind is spinning, and all I caught is that back home there is trouble. Fire in the mountains is never good, but fire in the mountains in the driest year on record for a hundred years is deadly.

Katie is quickly by my side, tears

streaming down her face. I turn to Rex, and he looks at me like he is reaching to grab onto my soul as he squeezes my hand, "Ember, it was the Greene Family ranch. Your family. They're all gone. I am sorry." Rex says it out loud again.

I pull my hand away from Rex and stand to walk away. I can't believe he would say something like that after not seeing me for years. I turn to confront them, "Chief, this isn't funny! Why would you say that? Momma just emailed me asking about the cruise." I turn away from Katie and Rex as my eyes are starting to water, and I am not sure what to think at this moment. I walk out to the balcony and peer up at the sky. There are no clouds in sight, just the waning moon and the stars starting to come out; it hits me in the gut and reminds me of home.

"Chief? I will take care of her. I will have her call…" Rex's voice fades into the distance as everything just said starts to hit me. This must be a dream. *Wake up, Ember!*

Katie stands beside me and wraps her arm around my waist, "Em, honey, I am so sorry. What can I do?"

"I need water," it's all I can say. She walks back into the cabin.

Rex is standing behind me now. He

doesn't touch me, but I feel his presence stop just short of doing so. A moment goes by before his hand gently touches my shoulder. He gently tugs on it and begrudgingly I turn around, he is standing closer to me than he has ever been in the entire time I have known him. My heart pounds so hard it feels like it might crack my ribs. He reaches down gently to take my hands, and even though they're trembling, I let him pull me closer to him. His eyes were full of tears again. He releases a deep breath before he starts talking.

"Em, … Chief Warren, he called me just a few minutes before we were supposed to meet, so did my mom. They wanted to know if I knew where you were, and I told him that I did. Em, I am so, so, sorry."

I look harder at Rex and really see him. There's steel in his features, but there is also hurt, despair, loss, grief, and so many other emotions on his face that I have never seen before. When his eyes betray him and the tears start to fall, something breaks inside me, and then the words he's been speaking suddenly hit me. Like a freight train.

"No, Rex!" I push him away from me, but he doesn't move, he just absorbs the touch. "No. They can't be gone…." I collapse into myself and start to crumble to the floor. Rex's arms catch me as I'm falling, and we hit the deck together. Someone nearby starts screaming. Rex starts speaking softly to me between his own tears, but I don't understand him over the screaming.

Oh God, that's me. I am screaming.

My chest gets tight and an ache that I have never felt before takes over in my chest. The pain is too big for words, and too loud for silence.

They're gone. All of them.

Chapter 6
The Stones Remember

5 years later

EMBER

The wind stirred the tall grass in lazy waves as the helicopter descended into the pasture on Greene Family Ranch. The rotors kicking up dust and memories I still wasn't sure I was ready to face, even after all this time. I kept my eyes on the ground, jaw clenched, one hand wrapped tight around the frayed leather strap of my bag. The smell of churned earth, dry hay, and pine hit me as the skids touched down; the valley had always smelled like this.

Katie's dad was the first to slide the door open, his grey hair moving wildly in the rotor spin-down. "You okay, Ember?" he asked me, concern on his face.

I didn't answer right away, just looked at the land before me, the ridge in the distance, and felt the way my heart ached. I hadn't stepped foot on this land in five years, not since the fire.

I nodded at Katie's dad, Jackson, before reaching for the hand he extended to help me exit the helicopter. As my western boots hit the grass, it felt foreign but also like home. I belonged here, but I was also not sure that I did. I took one look around and nearly crumbled.

The fire had gutted the valley, eaten the hillsides, and left behind bones; like death itself had swept the land. But now, five years later, the ranch had a different face. The blackened scars were there if you knew where to look — skeletal trees on the ridge, their bony fingers reaching for the sky. Gray stumps lining the gulch, where some trees had been cut down. Over time the damage had softened on the land.

The grass had returned, tall and golden-green. Aspens had crept back, their leaves flickering like old secrets. The pasture had healed, mostly. The deep pain in my chest though was not something I ever thought would heal. The fire took things that could never be replaced.

The new house didn't stand where the old one had burnt down. When I decided to come home, I had asked for the location of the house to be moved down the slope, closer to the lower pasture. It is still hidden from the beaten path but no longer tucked so far into the hillside that emergency crews couldn't reach it. The fire chief had said the original location was part of the reason why no one made it out. Besides, I couldn't bear to rebuild it there. This new house didn't try to mimic what was lost, but it did honor it. The thought lingered and my fingers curled tighter around my strap.

Jackson assists Katie from the helicopter

then turns to take in the ranch like he hasn't been here before, even though he personally assisted with the architecture, rebuilding, and design. He's tall and solid in his pressed jeans and tailored shirt, somehow still dignified even climbing out of a helicopter. He looked around like he was inspecting one of his southern mansions, but when he turned to me, his eyes were soft.

"We built it exactly how you asked, Ember. Every stone, every board."

I nodded, my throat tight. "I know. Thank you."

Katie slid an arm around my waist. "We brought something for you too, sugar. A housewarming gift."

Jackson moved us toward the porch, where a box sat waiting on the steps. Inside it, I later found a hand-carved sign with the ranch's name—Greene Family Ranch—burned into reclaimed barnwood, a new coffee percolator, and a custom keyring with my monogram on it; I was sure Katie had something to do with that last one.

I didn't have it in me to cry. Not yet.

Jackson walked me through the house while Katie trailed behind, silent for once. I barely heard the explanations. All I could see was the fireplace that stood in the middle of the house.

Many of the stones from the old house had been cleaned, restored, and reused with reverence. Not all had survived the fire, but the ones that had were set in place like a testimony to the history of what stood here before.

Above the hearth hung a photograph. A moment with all of us, frozen in time.

It had been taken on that camping trip when Tommy was a senior — when Tommy and Rex were both seniors. My parents arm-in-arm, Rex and Tommy grinning in the back row, Sally making a silly face, my uncle and grandparents being their normal selves with the addition of some bunny ears, and the ranch hands all lined up with dusty boots and smirks. I hadn't even known someone had captured that shot. Katie must've found it, had it blown up and framed. It was a perfect moment in time, and now they were gone.

I gasped, trying not to cry, and struggling to hold it in. It took all my strength not to crumble.

When I spoke, my voice sounded like gravel. "The safe room?"

Jackson's nod was solemn. "It's in the barn. Built just like you drew it. Ventilated, concrete lined. There's food storage for 72 hours, an emergency radio, benches, and a fold out cot if you need to sleep there."

I nodded. I wasn't sure if I would need it, but it was there if I did.

They stayed with me a while as I walked through the house taking in all the details. The open concept living area, the deep soaking tub, and the new furniture that was delivered and set up so that I wouldn't have to. Jackson, his wife Minnie, and Katie had helped me through every step of this process; they tried to make it easy for me.

When it came time for them to go, Katie hesitated. "You really don't want to go into town? Not even for groceries?"

I shook my head. "Not yet. I just... want space and time."

Jackson placed a hand on my shoulder. "We'll check in, but call us if you need us. Buck will be here by mid-week. We'll bring Misty later; she's not much of a puppy anymore. She's already learning the basics, but we figured you might want a few days to settle in before letting her loose. Misty's smart, Ember. A sheepdog through and through. She'll be ready when the flock comes. And if you need anything —"

"You'll bring it," I said softly. "I know. Thank you."

"You sure you don't want me to stay tonight, sugar?" Katie asks. She's asked no less than a dozen times now, but I know that I need to do this for me.

"Not tonight. But when you come back with Misty, plan to stay a few days." I smile as I hug her.

"You got it. Love you girl!" Katie turns to where Jackson is waiting, and they board the chopper. She waves to me from her seat, but I didn't wave back. I hadn't been able to say goodbye to anyone in five years, afraid that if I did, I would never see them again.

Standing there alone on the porch, the silence between the valley and the mountains was the loudest thing I had heard in years.

I wandered the property for a while, touching fence posts, brushing my fingers over the barn door, watching the cattle in the upper field—someone else's, for now. Sheep would come later. The land was green again. But the shadows remained.

Inside the new house, the air still smelled of fresh lumber and cut stone. I closed the door behind me and stood in the foyer, my boots echoing on the clean wood floors. This was supposed to be a home.

I wasn't sure if I could ever call it that again.

I made my way to the desk near the window, the one facing the pasture. From my bag, I pulled out my family Bible. The leather of the cover was cracked, the edges of the book were singed, but the pages inside were soft from generations of hands that came before me. It falls open and I ran my thumb over my daddy's notes in the margins.

"I'm not ready," I whispered, as if they were listening. I opened the bottom drawer of the desk and slid the Bible in before closing it.

I turned to the fireplace. The photo above seemed to watch me, but I stared back. I sat down on the couch that faced the mantel; it would have been a perfect picture for all of us to sit here and reminisce about. But that would never happen again.

"I don't know if this helps or hurts," I said to the picture, to the room, and to the land if it was listening. My voice cracked, "But I'm here. I came back."

The only answer was the wind outside. Then I broke. The tears I had held in since I boarded the chopper crashed over me like an avalanche. I sank to the floor in front of the hearth, sobbing into my hands.

"Why, God? Why did You let me live? Why them? Why not me?" I yelled the questions to the roof, like I could see straight to the gates of heaven. "You let them die! Why!?"

No answer came. Just like the last five years, silence. I was utterly alone.

The comfort of the couch beneath me, the softness of the blanket nearby — these things didn't answer, but they didn't leave me, either.

And that was something.

Eventually, my breathing slowed. The light shifted on the walls in the sunset. I stood and walked to the kitchen, poured myself a glass of water, and let it sit on the counter untouched.

Out the window, the pasture stretched wide and quiet, the mountains beyond cloaked in blue.

The ranch, the house, the land was mine, but I would have to make it a home.

I just wasn't sure if I was up for the challenge.

Chapter 7
Through Smoke & Song

REX

Ash still clung to the collar of my jacket when the truck pulled into the bay. The Stony Park fire had started like so many others — dry lightning and a strong wind — but this one turned in seconds. I had jumped in with my partner, Mitch Johnson, the wind at our backs, thinking we had the upper hand. Then the wind shifted.

Flames leapt sideways across the high California ridge, narrowing our escape route and consuming the line we'd spent all day cutting. We fought shoulder to shoulder, sweat stinging our eyes, lungs burning with smoke. Just when I thought we needed to evacuate, a sound carried through the fire— a low, steady singing. Voices in unison. Deep and grounded. Almost angelic.

Out of the smoke came a crew of Samoan firefighters, big men moving like shadows through the haze. Their chants rose above the roar of the fire—songs of strength and spirit. I didn't know the words, but some of the melodies were familiar, like hymns I'd grown up hearing. Melodies that sink into your soul and no matter how much time passes when you hear it, you know the song even if you forgot the words. The rhythm calmed the panic in my chest, giving my hands something steady to grip and a rhythm to follow. Together, the crew helped Mitch and I beat back the fire line inch by inch until it was finally under control.

God sent an army of angels that day, singing ones that fought fire. When I asked them about it later, one of the firefighters said that singing was part of their culture, but it also allowed them to stay motivated through the physically demanding tasks they face. I couldn't disagree with that. For Mitch and me, the songs had been infectious positivity; sometimes I still hear them.

It's been fourteen days since we went into the Stony Park fire. It's been hard and rewarding work, but I am ready for a break.

I stepped down off the fire rig before coming to lean against it for a moment. Aches in my muscles, sweat dried to my shirt, and I am sure I smelled like smoke and exhaustion. Around me, the rest of the crew from Bear Valley Fire Department piled out, their banter loose with relief.

"Smoke, you alive back there?" Mitch called, tossing his helmet into the bin. The Tennessee twang in Mitch's voice ringing in the oversize garage.

I gave a dry chuckle. "Barely. You guys ever going to give up calling me Smoke?"

Almost in unison the team retorted, "Nah!"

I just laughed as the other firemen made their way out of the truck and into the firehouse, the familiar smells of old reheated coffee and pine floor wax meeting us. I peeled off my jacket and dropped my gear into my locker.

I found a spot on the bench, tilted my head back and dozed off unexpectedly; the songs from the Samoan firefighters lingering in my ears.

As we gathered around the table that night, twelve of us eating lasagna, salad, and brownies that one of the wives had dropped off, it was nice to enjoy a last evening together with these men I called my brothers.

"You still headed out next week?" one of the rookies asked, shoveling a bite of lasagna into his mouth like he hadn't eaten in a week, and in some ways he likely hadn't.

I nodded. "Yeah. My mom's been asking for help around the place. Docs say she needs to take it easy for a while. I told her I'd stay through winter, maybe longer."

"When are you coming back?" another asked.

"I don't know. Need to see how she does and how long she needs me." I said looking around the large table at all of them, and Mitch leaning against the counter nearby.

"Big Montana sky. Mountains as far as the eye can see. Gotta get back to those roots?" Mitch asks. I will miss him the most. We had developed a deep friendship over the years. First in the military, and now here in the fire station. He had been the one to tell me about smoke jumping. I owed him a debt of thanks; it had helped me keep moving.

"Something like that," I replied, but my voice didn't carry the certainty I wished it did.

I hadn't said anything about the real reason I couldn't stop thinking about Montana lately. It wasn't just mom, it was also the land, the air, the peace. And Ember.

I hadn't seen her in five years. Not since that day Katie and her dad pulled up to take Ember back to college. Ember had barely looked at me. Barely acknowledged that she was leaving.

I sent her letters, but they always came back unopened. No forwarding address. No explanation.

I stood up from the dinner table and walked to the second-floor patio. Leaning on the railing, my head dropped forward, and my eyes closed. I could still hear the sound of her laugh dancing over the water the day we shared during the cruise. The way she smiled as we sat on the back of the ship sharing stories that neither of us had ever told anyone else. Her face lit up in a way I hadn't seen before or since. We'd even shared mutual hidden feelings about the other: sweet, honest, and raw.

And then with one call her world changed, and she disappeared.

I'd gone on to smoke jumper school, trained, served, jumped into fires from planes and wrestled wildfire from above. Meanwhile she'd gone back to college and graduated, but then from there — I didn't know where she went

But I never forgot her, never stopped thinking about her, and I never stopped praying for her.

Mitch slapped me on the shoulder, his heavy hand resting there and bringing me back to reality, "You good, man?"

"Yeah," I said, standing. "Just tired."

My mind was 1,000 miles away, climbing a fence line, walking a field with aspen at the edges, standing on the porch of a house that didn't exist anymore.

I wondered if she ever went back home. Did she still think about the ranch? Did she ever think about me? Was she still buried in grief?

I hadn't asked Katie. I couldn't. The last time I brought Ember up, Katie just said, "She's not ready, Rex." That was years ago now.

I honestly didn't know if she was ever going to be.

I went back in and finished dinner before I headed for the bunk room, where my duffel bag sat packed. I hadn't told anyone yet, but I knew I would probably have to file for extended leave. It wasn't a vacation. It was a reckoning.

I needed to go home. For mom. For me. For all that was lost years ago.

The sun was rising over the parking lot when I stepped outside, casting the world in gold. I squinted toward the light, my heart tugged east.

Montana was calling.

And I planned to answer.

Chapter 8
Smoke in the Valley

EMBER

It's been a year since I came back to the ranch—since I stood in this pasture with Jackson and Katie standing beside me. In that time, I've worked, I've grieved, and slowly I have started to heal. I don't think it will ever go away completely, but I am working on it.

This is no longer a cattle ranch; I've shifted to sheep. They are smaller, quieter, and easier for one person to manage—they're also

73

good in the cold. Misty's fully grown, trained to herd, and sharp as ever — just like Jackson said she would be. Buck's adjusted well too, his steady presence is a comfort I didn't know I needed. I have also added three more horses, but Buck's my best one.

The house feels more like a home now too. I have filled the walls with my things, not just my grief — but something still feels like it is missing. Something warm, like laughter and new memories. I'm not sure how to invite that in yet, but lately I've been wondering if I should.

Katie and Jackson visited six days ago and brought fresh supplies; I still don't have the nerve to go into town and face people. I tried once. Got my truck to the edge of town, then Mrs. Percy went by. She didn't recognize me, but I recognized her, the town gossip. I panicked and turned around and came right back to the ranch.

I have gotten used to the silence. Well, it's not really silence, the animals make a lot of sounds, but they don't judge. It's a controllable peace. Tentative and possibly not even real, but easier to deal with than judgment.

Katie's never judged me. She stood by my side, held my hand, and did all the things that a friend should do. Her and her family have been a blessing in my life. Jackson helped me get through probate and made sure I set myself up for success on the ranch, he also made sure that the land is in a trust that will go to wilderness conservation should something happen to me. I don't want the ranch to become subdivided plots. Moose Hollow's grown tremendously since I went to college and now those little neighborhoods are popping up everywhere.

I have two ranch hands that help when needed, Luke and Don. Technically they work for Katie's family, but they come here to drop off mail, run deliveries, and assist when there is something that I can't do on my own. They came up from North Carolina with Jackson's business. They're loyal to the Darling family, and now to me too; they don't talk about me to anyone they meet.

Wildfires in Canada have been burning fierce and the air in Montana is full of a yellow-grey haze this year. The winds blow the smoke into the valley where it sits waiting for the next gust of wind to blow it across the next ridge.

As I look toward the northern ridge I notice a heavy plume of smoke just starting to rise a few miles out. It's not close yet, but after all I have learned about fire, I know it doesn't take much to make a fire roar and thunder through the Bitterroot Mountains.

Buck lets out a neigh and I look in his direction. Coming up the road is a jeep, followed by a cloud of dust. Whoever is coming it still at least five minutes out, but they will be here soon. I am not expecting anyone, but maybe Katie's coming for a visit in a new jeep; she's been looking at one for a while now.

I head inside to pour myself a glass of sweet tea, a holdover from college that stuck. It always hits the tongue exactly right when I am parched. In the dry heat of mid-July in Montana, it's a treat.

I go to my desk and open the center drawer and take out a gun that I always keep close by. I don't feel threatened, but a woman alone on a ranch in the middle of Montana, and a car coming up the road that I don't recognize— I would rather err on the side of caution. I glance out the window and see that the jeep is almost here.

I am headed to the front door when I hear the vehicle door close, I take a deep breath before I open it. When I step onto the porch I am surprised to see the man standing before me.

"Ember," he tips his cowboy hat at me as he rests his boot on the first step of the porch.

"Chief Warren. How can I help you?" I say with a smile. At least it's someone I know, even if seeing him brings back memories I want to avoid.

"It's good to see you girl," he looks around a moment, taking in the changes, the growth, and what I am sure are cautious eyes looking for risk. "The ranch looks good; your family would be proud. I just came by to check and see if what I heard was true."

"Well, that depends on what you heard, Chief." I take a drink of my tea and wait for his response.

"You know my wife works for the county records office. She saw that a trust had applied for permits for the ranch and mentioned that something was going on out here. She said there's been a whole lot of secrets about what it was. I wanted to make sure that your family's ranch, and anyone here was ok. But I honestly didn't expect to find you here."

"I would really like to keep it that way,

please. I have gotten used to being here alone."

"Well, I guess if you are going to be stuck somewhere alone, being here in one of the most beautiful places God created is the place to be." He shifts his weight then, "Listen, Ember, I will keep this as quiet as I can. I won't tell anyone you're here. But," he gives me that looks that says whatever comes next is not optional, "there are two instances when that will not apply. One, if you call me and say you're in trouble. Two, if I call you and tell you that you are in trouble. Is that a deal?"

I look at him for a moment, then look around the ranch. It's two hundred acres of quiet, serene, secluded mountain land, twenty miles from the closest town, and often cell signals don't work out here. He has a valid point, and I know that my daddy would want me to be safe.

"Alright, Chief. I can agree with that." I put out my hand to shake on it, old fashioned like my dad did.

"No ma'am, that's not going to work. Come here kid." Chief Warren steps up and pulls me into a hug, and I don't resist. I have known him since I was born; he and my daddy were close friends.

When I pull away I look him in the eye and smile gently, "Thank you, for keeping my secret."

"I don't like it, but I do understand it. I know it's been years now, but we still talk about your family all the time. They meant a lot to this community and always will." He takes a deep breath, looks around the ranch a second time, then back at me, "You don't have to be alone Ember. You are missed too. There are people that want to know how you're doing, and a lot of people want to know if you're okay."

Chief Warren takes a business card out of his pocket and uses a pen from his breast pocket to scratch something down before handing it to me.

"This is my personal phone, and Margaret's. I will tell her to quash the gossip as she can. You call us anytime, Ember. I will answer." He tips his hat at me again before turning to leave.

I stand on the porch watching the jeep drive down the long road back to town. I don't remember much about the funeral, but I remember Chief Warren and his wife being there and checking on me after. He had told Rex to let him know how I was doing as time went on, Rex promised he would. Too bad I cut Rex out of my life for him to be able to do that.

I take a seat in the porch swing and watch as the sun glows the color of blood orange as it starts to set beyond the western ridge. The smoke from the Canadian fires hangs in the air and distorts the sunset, just like Chief Warrens words hang in my mind and distort the feelings of my heart.

Maybe it is time to start thinking about trying to connect with people again. The only way things are going to change is if I blow the smoke out of the valley and climb the mountain.

I step down onto the porch and the boards creak beneath my feet, as if encouraging the first steps forward.

Chapter 9
The Black Zone

REX

Fire changes everything.

It devours whatever lies in its path, changes the landscape, and makes its own rules. The worst part isn't the flames though; it's the silence that comes after. The black zone. That's where you learn what's left. That's where you find out who you really are.

From the open cargo door, I stare at the

ridge below, smoke curling up in layers like dirty cotton. From this height, it could be mistaken for almost peaceful. But I know better. I've jumped enough of these the last six years to know the difference between a fire you can fight and one you just have to survive.

Montana's burning up this year with more fires this summer than in the last five combined. It's drier than it should be and hotter than it ought to be.

Unofficially, a reckless camper who did not follow the posted fire rules for no open flames started the Blacktail fire, but it's the gusty winds that are doing real damage now as it jumps from ridge to ridge with zero containment. In Montana it feels like the wind blows every day of the year, and when the winds blow, the fires rage.

Standing here watching the world below pass by, my hand rests on my parachute harness, fingers flexing out of habit as I process the mission. Through the breaks in the smoke, I can barely make out the terrain below.

It's funny how life has a way of circling back. I jumped out of planes for the military because I thought war was the hardest thing I'd ever do. Turns out, fighting fire is harder. The flames don't negotiate, don't blink, and it doesn't give you time to think about regrets.

That's why I like it. I have a lot of regrets.

"Blacktail Ridge," the pilot calls through the headset. "Five minutes to drop."

I make eye contact with the other smoke jumpers prepared to drop at separate locations, but it's just Mitch and I jumping in five. He and I nod, mostly at each other since the pilot couldn't see us. Mitch, my jump partner from California, moved to Montana shortly after I made my move permanent. Said he needed to see what all the raucous was about for himself; it's been nice to have him here.

The plane bounces but I am steady on my feet. My heart's already slowing down, not speeding up. That's the part most people don't understand. The closer I get to the jump, the calmer I get. This is the place where nothing else matters. Just the ground below, the fire, and the mission.

And today's jump is one I am familiar with. I grew up playing in the shadows of Blacktail Ridge on the far side of the Greene Family Ranch. Running on its dirt roads, swimming in its creeks, and doing all the things Montana ranch kids do. That was before the military and before the fire six years ago claimed the lives of the family there. All but one, Ember.

The ranch had been settled in the 1800s when Ember's great-great-grandfather came to Montana on the railroad. When the trains stopped coming as often, the family switched to raising cattle and growing the crops they could in Montana's high country. They had created a life that most could only dream of, until a lightning storm lit up the mountainside and the sparks became a blaze fueled by wind.

Ember only survived because she wasn't here. She was on a ship in the ocean, with me.

Guilt had riddled me for years about it. Knowing that I had been spending time with that same best friend's little sister, that I had run into by happenstance at the ship's club, and I had been getting ready to take her out for dinner that night and admit my feelings for her.

Ember had always been off limits; Tommy had made that well known. But I had been attracted to her for years, her mind, her body, and her soul. I had hoped she would give me a chance then. But the tides changed, and the wind shifted with one call from Chief Warren that they were all gone.

The Greene Family Ranch is remote and

hard to traverse to, so when the fire raged, the family didn't even have time to leave. Chief Warren later told me that they found most of the family members in vehicles that burned out on the roads, trapped between downed trees. Two other family members were found in the fields near the dead livestock, and one, my best friend Tommy, was near the house. Likely he had tried to wet it all down to save it, but the fire consumed everything in its path.

All that was left was Ember, and that stubborn horse they found days later, Buck. A rancher nearby found him wandering along the riverbank headed towards home.

That night on the ship, when Chief Warren called me, I knew something had happened; I never imagined just how bad it truly was. It didn't hit her immediately that they were gone, but when the truth set in, that they were … she cried and screamed. It was like nothing I have ever heard from another human being, even in war.

I carried her to bed that night. Somewhere in the hours that followed, Ember's voice gave out before her sobs did, her throat raw from screaming. Katie called the ship's doctor to give her something to relax her for the remainder of the trip. When we made it to port the next day, Katie and I took her home to Montana, or what was left of it.

I put her up at my mom's house and stayed around to help her out with anything she needed. Afterall, I knew her family as well as if they were my own. In many ways they were since mom and I had lived on the ranch for most of my life. Mr. Greene, Ember's Dad, had poured into me over the years. My father had died when I was a baby, so the only father figure I had growing up, was Tommy and Ember's dad.

After a few weeks Katie came and took Ember back to North Carolina for her senior year of college. I hoped that returning to school and routine would be good for Ember. But letting her go, seeing how catatonic she was, was like ripping out my heart and watching it leave. Shortly after that I started smoke jumper school.

I called her daily, but she didn't talk, so I just talked to her about my day, my job, and anything else I could think of telling her. Eventually, she stopped answering. At first, I told myself she just needed space. But the silence between us stretched longer and deeper, and eventually even Katie stopped picking up the phone too. That's when I started writing letters, but they were all sent back, marked "return to sender." After a while, I stopped trying. But I continued to pray for her every day, same as that night on the ship, whispering a prayer into the wind before everything changed.

I heard Em finished college that year, graduated with honors, but that was the last anyone heard from her. She was supposed to go to veterinary school after that, but no one knows if she did. It's like she just disappeared. Like she was there at the ranch the day the fire came through and went with them, but she wasn't.

The plane banks hard left, and I am pulled back to the fire at hand, but the smoke of the fire long gone still lingers. Looking out the back of the plane, I see that the old fire burn scar is mostly gone now, but the remnants of damage are still there.

Mitch looks at me and tilts his head. As my partner for the last few years, I know he sees the flames I am fighting inside, but I give him a thumbs up. He's wary, I can see it in his eyes, but he gives me a thumbs up back. Mitch followed me to Montana when a position opened for a smoke jumper. And it worked out for us both that we already had history together in California wildfires.

Jumping onto the ridge that I grew up on, where the Greene's died, to help fight a fire that is threatening to spread again to the ranch and beyond... it's like fighting an emotional zombie fire; it's burning beneath the surface, you just can't see it. When it comes to the surface, it's going to burn.

I roll my neck, clear my head, adjust my gear, and check my altimeter, my harness, and my helmet again. Secure and ready to go. That's the thing about smoke jumping. You always have to be ready. Fire doesn't wait.

This jump, I have a feeling it won't be the fires I can see waiting on the ridge. This time the fires that lay quietly beneath the surface might just become a blaze.

Chapter 10
Hold Fast

EMBER

The fire I saw burning several days ago a few ridges over is coming closer to my ranch, fast. The late summer Chinook winds are blowing hard. Nothing new, but during fire season, that's bad news.

This fire was completely avoidable, but one reckless decision by someone not paying attention to fire warnings was now wreaking havoc across the Bitterroot Mountains, and fast.

Several ranches, businesses, and one small town have already been consumed from what I heard on the news.

I started preparing the ranch the same day that I saw smoke rising in the distance. Pulling away fuel, loading water buckets, and running hoses from the water spigots to wet down the land around the house and barn.

But now the fire's getting closer by the minute. I worked all day yesterday until I was bone tired. This morning, I started out at sunrise, working through ash and sweat, and I can feel every hour of it in my bones. To save what I rebuilt. To save what's left after the fire took so much from me six years ago.

Watching the smoke blowing into the valley get thicker and thicker, it's making me second guess coming back here. Like the fire nearby is reigniting all my fear, pain, and locking my heart back up. Just when I was considering taking a step back toward trying to have a life.

Chief Warren just radioed in that he is sending in a rescue team, but I am not leaving. I know I told him I would go, but this is my home.

My family members had been born here,

married here, and died here. They're all buried here, right up on the mountain side, overlooking the valley. That's where I had started pulling back vegetation first, the cemetery.

In all there are 46 members of my family buried on this ranch. Some members of the Greene family that were born here never left. Some of them never even left Montana, except for three. A great aunt, an uncle, and me. The great aunt moved to Seattle at 18 and never came back, not even to visit. My grandmother said they had a falling out but never said over what.

My uncle had left to attend college before returning to Montana with a family in tow; a young wife and son. They had only been back a short while before the fire that took their lives.

Before the fire, I didn't think that I would ever come back. I was happy traveling the world, meeting new people, and experiencing life at a different pace than this ranch had to offer me.

That cruise changed everything — and seeing Rex again, even briefly, made the loss feel sharper somehow, like the good things were just as out of reach as the ones I buried. Then when they were gone, I didn't want to be here anymore. When Katie came and took me back to school, it was a good thing. I needed the routine and structure, and my college friends drug me everywhere, like they were afraid to leave me alone. It wasn't until after vet school that I came back.

Buck neighs from the fence line across the ranch and I look up. The ridge is getting darker as the smoke moves across the valley. "I know Buck, I am moving." I had already removed his bridle, opened the pen, and let the animals have full run of the ranch, but Buck stayed close when the other horses left. I have a feeling he won't leave unless I do.

Over by the creek, Misty has the sheep corralled in. They're hunkered down for now, but I know she will move them if she needs to. Misty was gifted to me by Katie and her parents. They knew I was coming home and said I would need a companion, as well as a sheep dog. My family had run cattle all these generations, but it's just me now, so sheep it is.

Katie had called two nights ago and asked how I was; I told her I was fine. Her and Jackson are in Europe on tour for her Minnie's new book. They won't be back in the states for a few more weeks. I assured Katie I would leave the ranch if the fire got close, but here I am.

I have pulled back anything that will burn near the house, the barn, and the shed where I store hay. If I lose the shed, I can replace the hay, but the house and barn were rebuilt a year ago. I don't want to lose those.

My leather gloves are thick with sweat when I pull them off. I slide them in my back pocket before heading into the house to refill my water bottle, secure some valuable documents, and drop a load in the fire shelter. The water's been running all day from every spigot on the outside of the house and barn. I don't want to disrupt the water pressure, so I grab bottled water instead. I dump it into my canteen and clip it on my hip.

In the office I open the desk drawer to find the documents and put them in a bag with a few more bottles of water that I am dropping in the fire shelter. As I am picking the documents up from the drawer my fingertips brush leather. There under the birth certificates, death certificates, and my diploma is my great grandfathers family bible. Even with the sears on the edges, somehow the contents remained unburned in the last fire. Momma always said the Word would outlast the flames, that even when the world burned, God's promises wouldn't. When the firemen brought it to me before the funeral, I couldn't believe it had made it. It was one of the only things that did.

I pick it up and thumb through the pages quickly. I haven't opened a bible or been to church since their funerals. It feels strange holding this bible, knowing the stories it could tell. I flip to the front page where births, marriages, and deaths have been recorded for the last six generations. Only two dates haven't been filled in, me and my great-aunt. With the fire nearby, I am not sure who's date will go in next.

I forgot the old Bible was even in my desk, but now that I have it in my hands, I can't leave it behind. I might still be working through things, but I know Jesus is my savior and my momma would not want me to leave this behind. I flip to her favorite verse Isaiah 41:10, *So do not fear, for I am with you; do not be dismayed, for I am your God. I will strengthen you and help you; I will uphold you with my righteous right hand.* I see her notes written next to it, her perfect cursive that I had longed to be able to mimic, "Not alone. Not Forgotten. Not unloved." Next to her note, a small heart drawn in, just like the ones she would lean over and put on my notes—an "I love you" just between us.

Quickly I close the Bible before the tears start to fall. A knot forms in my throat, thick and aching, and I force myself to swallow it down. *Not now, Ember.* I pull the old Bible close to my chest for a moment before sliding it into my drop bag and heading out the door.

Walking across the yard to the barn I remember that I need to chase the chickens off before they get too scared to leave. I had already pushed them out of their pen and closed it behind them so they can't get back inside. I can pull Misty away from the sheep long enough to help, I want to try to force them to the creek too.

Whistling as I walk, Misty perks up and looks at me. She thinks twice, looking back at her sheep, then back to me, then comes running. When she gets to me, she turns to look for her sheep, "Eyes here girl," I talk to her like she's human as we start walking toward the chickens. She kind of is human to me since she's the only one here and the only one I talk to anymore. "We need to get the chickens moved out of here, near the creek. All the pens are locked up, so they have nowhere to go. Let's get this done." Misty looks up at me as if to say *got it* before she takes off.

She swiftly crosses the space but then approaches the chickens with caution, knowing they will scatter if scared. She gets down on all fours and points them in the direction she wants them to go. Every few minutes she moves spots, always cautious, but intense. I don't have time to stand and watch; I still have more fire line to dig. There's a natural break where the creek is on the south side, and then another where the boulders stand up out of the land on the east, but north and west are the issue.

The house is surrounded by fire line I have already cut, but the barn and shed are still incomplete. As I look up at the ridge to gauge the fire and wind, I see an ember falling from the sky. It hits the ground and glows bright, pulsing red and orange. For a moment I stop and watch it, the color changing like its breathing every few seconds. I feel like that; sometimes I still have to remind myself to breathe — and remember who gave me breath. No time for poetic pleasantries now.

I step on the ember to extinguish it before it does more damage.

There's fire line to dig.

Chapter 11
The Jump

REX

The jump plane rattles beneath me, the wings bending and flexing in the altitude and warm air. This is the part I live for, the edge of the jump door, right before gravity takes over. I look at Mitch, then tighten my harness and check my gear one last time. Altimeter set. Reserve clipped. Helmet snug. And a prayer.

My lips move silently as I tap the cross

beneath my shirt. *"Lord, it's me again. I am jumping into the fire today, and there are lives at stake beside my own. Help me to be aware of fire, wind, and what I can't see. Guide my chute and my feet to the landing zone. Help me dig quickly and assist anyone we come across that may be in need. Amen."*

Not for safety. Not for glory. For purpose.

Beneath us, the Blacktail Ridge fire rages across the Bitterroot Mountains. The ridges stretch out beneath us, but the sky's gone grey with smoke. The smoke glowing amber and orange where the flames reach toward the sky. Chinook wind is extra bad today. Real bad. The plane banks, circling the green zone again. It's hotter down there than it should be.

"Two minutes!" the spotter shouts holding up two fingers.

I give him a thumbs-up, but Mitch and I exchange a look. Something's off; we've been circling for too long.

The spotter hands me a headset. Crackling comes through the line.

"Smoke, change of orders. Johnson's drop point's moving south to Saddle Ridge. You're staying in Blacktail for a solo insertion."

My stomach knots. Smoke jumpers don't jump alone unless they have no choice, or a specific mission.

"Copy that," I say anyway. We don't argue orders up here.

"And, Smoke, we confirmed a civilian on the ground. It's Ember Greene. Chief Warren just talked to her. She's refused evac multiple times. I know you are familiar with her ranch, but it is right at the edge of the green zone. We are struggling to get equipment in due to its location. We need eyes on her. If you can get her out, do it. If not, keep her alive till ground crews get in."

"Say again?" I ask. I am not sure I heard that call right.

"You heard him right, Smoke. Ember's home. She's at the ranch, and she won't leave." Chief Warren's voice crackles through this time, I hear the concern in his tone.

99

"Copy." I hand the headset back to the spotter and give him and Mitch a thumbs up.

"Who's Ember Greene?" Mitch yells, the sound of the plane mostly drowning him out.

"That's a story for another day, Mitch. See you at the station." Mitch looks at me for a minute, then steps back from the door.

What the hell is Ember doing at the ranch? She's supposed to be in Vet school. How did she slip back into our hometown and no one notice?

Too many questions. This is no longer a job; this is now a mission. I need to find Ember, immediately.

The spotter gives the signal, the green light flashes, and I drop into the void. The wind blasts my face, but it's more like floating, then falling.

The first second of falling is silent, like the world dropped away. Then the smoke hits, curling around me, and swallowing me whole.

The square chute opens above me and

catches the wind with a jolt. With steering toggles in hand, I keep my canopy tight. No drift. Just precision. Below, the black zone stretches like scorched earth, skeletons of trees burned stabbing skyward, and the green zone, dry kindling waiting to blaze blows in waves beneath the gusty winds.

Usually this is peaceful and an adrenaline rush all at once. Today it's suddenly full of fear, and adrenaline doesn't behave when there is fear. Knowing that Ember is on the ground, I am worried, but fear is dangerous, so I control my breathing and focus.

As the ground moves closer to me, I take in all the details of the land that I can before losing any visual advantage. Through the smoke I spot where the ranch house used to be in the distance, it's still empty. But to my surprise, a new house has been built, as well as a barn, and another structure of some kind in the field nearby.

Ember's not just home; Ember's rebuilt.

As the earth gets closer, I prepare for impact in my landing zone. My boots hit hard, and I bend my knees to absorb the impact. Crouched, I unclip my chute and pack it fast. The air burns my throat, heat curling up from the ash. My goggles fog for a second when the temperature slams me, but they clear quickly.

Wind's shifting to the southwest. That's not good. I need to move fast.

I tap my radio. "Smoke, on the ground."

Static.

"Moose Hollow Fire, Smoke, confirmed on the ground."

Nothing. The terrain must be shielding my signal. Not the first time I have been alone, though.

Fear starts to creep back up; if they can't hear me, they can't hear calls from Ember either.

I shoulder my pack and grab my Pulaski tool before scanning the terrain again from the ground. The ridge slopes down into a smoke-filled valley, the ground blackened and slick with ash and falling embers. I pause for a second to take it all in, not just the fire, but the terrain itself.

Switchbacks cut down the slope like careful scars. The land here folds in on itself, full of creeks that run clear even now, the water threading through rocks and underbrush like it's the veins of the mountain. Thick groupings of pine cling to what ground the fire hasn't stolen, and the ranch rests so deep in this wild pocket of mountain that getting to it can be a challenge. It's the kind of place you only find if you know exactly where to look, and thank God, I know this land by heart.

I take in the perimeter and identify the most likely areas for the fire to run if the wind catches it. If I cut south, I can skirt the worst of the fuel, stay in the shadow of the ridgeline, and use the creek bed for cover if needed. It's slower, but safer. Just old, scorched timber and overgrown trail, but it's my best shot at reaching her quickly. If I can find her.

The new house I saw is about a mile from here, tucked against the base of the mountain, nearly invisible. From my viewpoint now, I see that there are more fallen trees that crisscross the slope like dead giants. Some of the downed trees are old, but some are new with plenty of dry tinder to ignite rapidly. I imagine that no one has been here to care for the ranch for years.

Regret hits me hard. I should've flown to North Carolina to check on her when she stopped responding. I should've come back here to the ranch to look when I came home last year. I should've kept calling, but I didn't. Now all the should haves that I missed are eating me alive. And I can't do that right now; I need to stay focused.

The ones who stay behind when everyone else evacuate are either stubborn, scared, or ready to die. Ember might be all three; after losing her family, she might feel like she has nothing to lose.

Feet steady, eyes sharp, I make my way toward the structures I saw from the air. That's the first place to start.

One step closer to a woman I should've fought harder for. A woman I have always harbored feelings for. Now I am on my way to her, and I hope I find her.

God willing, I won't fail her.

I crest the next small ridge and pause, squinting through the haze. Below me, about a hundred yards out, a small figure moves in the smoke. Through the haze in the shadows, it looks like they're cutting fire line around the barn.

Glancing further down the slope of the mountainside I see a small herd of sheep clustered together near the creek, a border collie keeping them hunkered down. There's also a beautiful Appaloosa running the fence line, the gate to the corral wide open and swinging in the wind. That thick grey streak in his tail tells me its Buck, the lone livestock survivor of the last fire.

When Buck came home days after the fire, he wouldn't let them wrangle him, he was determined to make it on his own. He didn't know there was no one or nothing there to go back to. He just knew where home was.

When we brought Ember home for the funerals, Ember stayed at my mom's house and a neighbor boarded Buck for as long as she needed. Ember never talked, just sat there. Occasionally she would nod her head to answer questions. Except for her daily walks with Buck, she barely moved.

Ember would go out to the stall where he was, put a lead on him, and walk with him along the perimeter of the neighbors ranch. He always walked at her pace, like he knew she needed him and maybe he also needed her; he lost his family that day too.

I would often spot them at the end of the fence looking in the direction of home. Ember would climb up on his back and lay onto his neck. The two of them would stand there for as long as it took. When she was ready, she would ride him bareback to the barn before spending hours brushing him. I let her have that time, she needed it.

After the summer passed, Katie took her back to North Carolina for college that fall, and Katie's dad, Jackson, had Buck moved south to be near Ember. That was the last time I saw him or her, until right now.

Closing the distance, I can see the figure

has a long red braid swinging down their back as they dig a fire line, Ember. She's wearing jeans, boots, and a faded yellow T-shirt. No helmet. No mask. Just a baseball hat, a bandana around her mouth and nose, and stubborn grit.

Watching her now, working on a fire line with steady hands and that same quiet resolve she's always had, I realize just how far she's come. Back then, she could barely stand without leaning on Buck. The girl who clung to a horse just to breathe is gone. In her place is this woman who doesn't flinch at smoke, who won't run—not this time.

Now, she stands in the middle of a green zone like she's daring the fire to come take her down. And that's what guts me the most. Because while she's hardened into something steel strong, I wonder if there's any part of her left that still feels safe enough to soften. Safe enough to let someone back in.

Looking around the property as I close the distance, I see that she has prepped for this fire the best she can. She's got fire hoses hooked to the house and barn, sprinklers spraying toward the barn roof, and fuel cleared back thirty feet from the house. It's well planned but it still won't be enough if the wind shifts in this direction.

I adjust my pack and start closing the distance between us. Ash floats in the air, coating my tongue with bitterness. The acrid scent of burnt pine and smoke clings to every breath. My pulse kicks up, not just from the conditions, but from seeing her. Ember, here, alive, and digging in with fierce determination like she's part of the mountain itself. She hasn't seen me yet, and for a moment I hesitate, watching her move with grit and grace through the haze, a red and yellow ember against a backdrop of ruin.

When I'm close enough to speak without shouting, I stop. No sudden moves. Fire's one thing, but surprising Ember is not something I want to do when she thinks she is alone.

"Em?"

Chapter 12
Hold the Line

REX

Ember whips around fast, eyes narrowing. Her hand hovers near her hip like she half expects trouble; she has her daddy's knife in her waist band. That instinct, that readiness doesn't surprise me, but it does gut me a little.

She's still the same fierce Ember, but more guarded now. Hardened. And yet, she still looks like the girl I never stopped watching from across the room.

"Rex!?" She rips the bandana off her face, her voice sharp but unsure. As if she's not sure if she is seeing me. "Why are you here? How did you get here?"

"Smoke jumper. Remember? Last time I saw you I was waiting for training to start." I pause a moment to let that sink in, and calmly say the next part, "I am here to get you out."

"Told the Chief I didn't need a rescue, *Rex*." She quickly turns her back to me and continues her work, but she keeps talking, "In case you missed it, the roads is not accessible, trees have fallen down everywhere, and quite frankly," she turns back to face me, her braid whipping around her shoulder, "I am not going. I *don't* need a rescue." She pulls her bandana back up and gets right back to work.

The ire in her voice tells me she honestly thinks she would be fine out here alone.

"Didn't say you did, Em." She does, but she's not willing to admit that. Stubborn?

Check.

I put down my pack and use my axe to start cutting line next to her. She looks over her shoulder just long enough to see that I am not getting in her way but contributing to what she's doing. She doesn't respond, doesn't smile, just keeps on moving.

The fire line we are digging encircles the barn and connects to the fire line she has already dug around the house. She's been busy and I can't help but wonder how long she has been at this? It's had to have been days.

We work for a solid hour before she stops. She grabs a nearby canteen and takes a drink, all the while sizing me up the same way I'm sizing her.

"Em..." I start cautiously.

"Don't 'Em' me." She puts her lid on her canteen, before turning back to her work again.

"Fine. *Ember*." I return the tone she used on me earlier. I shift my weight, keep my tone calm and step closer to her to work while talking to her. "Command sent me to check on

111

you. Fire's shifting. You're in the danger zone."

"I know where I am." She says it without a break, without a blink, and continues in her work.

Of course she knows she's in the danger zone. I imagine that she can't stand here on this land without thinking about it.

I take a moment to try to radio into base again, but there's still no signal, just crackle. "You have another radio?"

"Yep, but it sounds just like yours. Between the mountains and the fire, nothing's getting in or out."

Another thirty minutes pass before she steps away to take another drink. She looks me up and down again, like she is still trying to assess if I am going to throw her over my shoulder and run with her. As much as I would like to, I know she's been through hell, and truthfully, if the roads are blocked like she says, there is nowhere to go.

"Barn's got a safe room," she says before I can ask. "Had it put in when I rebuilt.

Reinforced walls, vented, and it's got enough supplies for seventy-two hours. If it gets too bad, we can take cover."

"Good," I say looking up at the ridge and watching the flames and smoke dance in the wind like a chaotic but beautiful ballet. "We might need it."

Most folks out here don't prepare, even the wildland office tells you that it's probably not worth it. But she lost everything to fire, and now I think she is taking a stand. That's what this is for her.

She looks at me, her face hardened. "I'm not leaving."

"I know. And I'm not asking you to, Em. At least not yet." I pick up my axe and get back to it.

She tilts her head and watches me for a minute. "You're staying?"

I nod, letting the sound of the steel slice the earth fill the space between us for a moment. "If you are not going, then yes, it looks like I am staying." Not just because I have orders. Not just because she's in danger. Because for the first time in years, I know exactly where I'm supposed to be, and it's beside her, in this fight, on this mountain. I failed her once by not being available. I won't make that mistake again.

We finish the remaining distance of the fire line around the barn, with two of us working it, it went quickly.

"We aren't going to be able to save the shed. It's going to have to burn if the fire comes," she says it out loud, but I don't think she is saying it to me; she just needed to say it for herself.

"Head back?" I ask as my eyes watch the flames and smoke on the mountainside.

"I want to walk the property line first." She looks at me then and I nod before I fall in at her pace.

Buck had joined us as we were cutting line and now walks the property line stationed behind Ember and me. There's a snag tree that I point out will come down if the wind shifts again. She listens but doesn't agree. I check the fuel breaks around the house, and I noticed where she cleared the brush. It's solid work but still may not be enough.

"Have you always been this stubborn?" I ask.

She glances at me sideways. "Have you always been this bossy?"

I almost smile. Almost.

"This isn't about bossing you, Ember," I say. "It's about staying alive. You and me. Anything you lose on this ranch can be replaced, except you." I meant it as a reminder, but I see the words land on her heart.

She huffs a breath, wiping sweat off her forehead, assessing the area around her. "You tell me that like I don't already know it."

"I tell you that to remind you what you're worth."

"Then we better get moving," she turns her back as she says it and starts walking away.

Buck has joined Misty and the other animals at the creek, his ears flicking, but keeping near the sheep.

"They're holding together," I say, trying to keep my voice steady.

"Yeah." Her throat works around the word. "They know what to do, especially Buck." She puts her axe over her shoulder and heads toward the fence line.

She lifts her axe and takes a swing at the fencepost holding the barbed wire in and connects with the wood. She swings repeatedly, and within five swings, the post gives away and the fence drops. Buck and Misty sense the change and move off the ranch; the other animals follow behind. They follow the creek, but they have room to run now if they need it.

Her gaze flicks to me, then back to the house and barn. She opens her mouth like she's about to say something but closes it again. A long pause stretches between us. The moment is heavy with words that are too hard to speak. Finally, in a voice rough with restraint, she says, "I didn't get them out in time."

"What do you mean?" I ask.

"Last night, I thought I'd load them up and move us off the mountain. I had the trailer hitched before the fire jumped the northernmost roads, but the tire blew on the truck as I headed down the mountain." Her jaw tightens. "I called Chief Warren, who said the team would be right out. He sent a crew up, but the wind had already taken trees down across the road. No one could get to me, and I couldn't get out. But I couldn't leave the animals alone, so I came back."

Ember looks in the direction of the road that leads to town. The same direction that the fire is bearing down on us from.

A strand of her red hair breaks loose from her braid and blows in the wind. I instinctively reach up to tuck it behind her ear. When I touch her, she startles but then looks at me for a moment.

It's just a second in time, but it suddenly feels like we are back on the ship. Ember looks like she is lost in the same memory. The moment is disrupted by the sound of a tree falling somewhere in the distance.

She turns away quickly, "We should keep moving." She steps away and heads toward the barn.

The fire burning in my chest can't decide if it just breathed fresh breath, or if it was just smothered.

Chapter 13
When the Wind Turns

EMBER

His touch was gentle, kind, and caught me off guard. For a moment I smelled the salt in the air and heard the sound of a live band playing steel drums. But that was then, and right now, I don't need any distractions.

Smoke curls at the edges of the sky like a warning. The flames in the distance are bright, flocking, and bitter; a harsh reminder of all I have lost.

I hear the static burst from Rex's radio, sharp and sudden. He straightens, holding it to his ear.

"Command, come again?" he says, voice tight.

But there's nothing else after that. Just more garbled crackle. No words. No directions. No warning. Only the sound of fire consuming timber somewhere beyond our view.

He lowers the radio slowly. "I got part of it. Sounded like a wind shift."

I don't need anyone to tell me that. Even without the fire, when the winds change in Montana, you feel it. And being this close to a fire, you feel the warmth shift as the flames change their mind. The air goes still, and that's when you know it's too late to get ahead of it.

We both turn toward the horizon. A wave of heat shimmers above the tree line distorting the tips of the trees with the sky above it. A plume of black curls upward. The fire's not just creeping anymore. It's running.

My hand clenches the shaft of my axe. My heart pounds in my ears. It's happening again.

We work side by side without speaking.

120

That's the only way to stay ahead of panic, keep moving. Rex cuts dry brush along the barn's back line while I drag the cleared fuel away from the structure.

It's too hot and dry, just like that summer six years ago.

My thoughts go back to the ship. Not the ocean breeze or the way Rex had looked at me like I was the only girl in the world. Not the moment I thought that maybe God was giving me something good.

No. I remember the stars above the glass dome at the staircase when I was waiting for Rex, the quiet hum of laughter that floated in the air, and then the way Rex's face looked as he ran toward me on the stairs.

I remember how his hands were shaking when he took mine. How his eyes filled with tears before he even spoke. I remember screaming.

The fire had hit while I was gone — while I was smiling, dancing, and *laughing*. With Rex. It took everything. My parents. My brother. My uncle and his family. My grandparents. Every living thing on the ranch, except for Buck. I wasn't there. I couldn't stop it.

I didn't even get to say goodbye. And I've been living my life with that regret and been searching for a way to make up for it ever since.

I drop the brush pile harder than I mean to. Rex turns toward me, concern written all over his face. I wave him off and keep moving. I won't break. Not again. Not with fire breathing down our necks and Rex standing beside me.

A little later, Rex and I stand side-by-side under the porch roof, scanning the horizon together.

The fire has crested the ridge. And it's beautiful in a way that makes my stomach twist. Red, orange, and gold bleeding into the now grey Montana sky; the blue hidden behind the smoke. Snag trees exploding from the inside, the smoke rising like a storm cloud with no mercy in it.

"That's coming straight for us," Rex says.

"Yeah." The wind licks at our backs now. From the wrong direction.

A distant hum cuts through the sky. We both look up as an air tanker passes overhead.

The big red belly opens and unleashes a stream of retardant—thick and wide, a red waterfall across the trees ahead of us.

It falls, but it doesn't make it to its intended target. A wind gust catches it, flinging it wide.

"Won't do much good if it doesn't hit the crown," Rex says. "They're stretched thin already. That is probably all we're getting."

I can't stop watching the line of flames as it starts to descend the slope. It's moving fast. The kind of speed that eats everything in its way, including people.

"We need to get to the water barrels," I say before quickly running to where I stationed the large plastic barrels at the base of the tree line just beyond the barn and house fire line.

Rex looks at me curiously. "What exactly are your intentions, Ember?"

"Soak the ground and hope the fire slows or diverts around it. Make it too wet to burn in this spot." I pick up my ax and lift it to swing. Rex takes a few steps back.

My shoulders pull back before I swing hard and put a large hole in the front of the first barrel, jimmy out my axe, then move down the line and continue, one barrel at a time. Rex nods then joins me in making holes in the oversize plastic barrels. The water starts to pour out in droves; it looks like a small tidal wave overtaking the hill side.

Within minutes the 15 barrels that I strategically placed are pouring water down the hill side in the direction of the house and barn. The water soaking everything in its path. I don't know if it will work, but it's worth a shot.

Rex steps next to me, and our shoulders brush. My throat tightens.

I didn't expect to see him again, not like this. Not when my hands are blistered and my heart is thudding like it might shake loose from my ribs. He's broader than I remember him. Fire's shaped both of us; we are different inside and out.

I hear Misty bark and look in her direction. She is leading the sheep into the creek, Buck behind them. They head down the far side of the bank, winding away from the direction of the fire.

"That's all I've got left," I whisper.

Rex doesn't pretend not to hear me, "You've got more than you think."

The words don't soothe me, but I don't argue. Not right now.

The wind shifts again, and it's getting hotter and stronger this time. The air goes from dry to suffocating. Smoke wraps around us like a hand closing in.

Rex removes his glove, drops to one knee, and presses his palm to the dirt. "It's warm." He looks up at me then, and I know it's time.

A crack echoes from the ridge behind the house. My head jerks up, so does Rex's.

We both see it at the same time— a massive tree, half-charred, teetering in the wind. Another gust hits it, stronger this time.

"Move!" he shouts.

The tree groans, leans, and begins to fall.

Chapter 14
Even in the Fire

REX

The moment the tree cracked loose, I knew it wasn't good, but I didn't expect it to roll. The burning tree hit the slope with a deep *thud*, and for a split second, I thought we were clear. But then the whole trunk shifted, and that massive, flaming pine started to move, straight toward us.

"Run!" I shout at Ember, already

reaching for her hand to drag her toward the barn.

We ran hard, boots slipping on ash and water, the slope turning slick and unstable as the wind howled down the mountain. Behind us, the burning tree barreled down like a judgment-day wrecking ball, spinning, and gaining momentum.

Each time the tree struck the ground, it flung sparks in every direction like a rogue firecracker. Dry brush caught instantly. Small trees ignited in the trees wake.

The fire line we cut earlier is gone in seconds.

The entire mountainside and ranch become chaos as sparks turned into flames. Heat raged and the smoke filled in around us. The fire we'd fought so hard to hold at bay had just leapt the line like it never existed.

I looked around assessing our options. As we continued down the hill, the tree was gaining on us, but I pulled Ember down and to the left behind a large boulder that jutted from the ground, wrapping myself around her. The tree bounced hard on the ground, before it passed us, missed the barn, and finally slammed into the creek at the bottom of the hill, hissing and steaming like oil on a hot cast iron pan. Water boiled around the trunk momentarily, the power of the water extinguishing the flames, but the damage to the land was already done.

What had been a manageable burn was now a fast-moving fire, and it was racing toward the barn, the house, and the north pasture, spurred by the small fires it engulfed as it moved. Everything we'd prepared was about to be assessed, and most of it wouldn't hold.

Ember coughed beside me, covering her mouth with her arm, but I see the tears hanging in her eyes. "Rex, I am going to lose the ranch again."

"I am here, Ember," I put my hand on the top of her arm, like I did before on the ship, anchoring her. "We are doing this together."

She looks at the flames. Her jaw is clenched, and her eyes open wide. Her whole body is shaking, not from fear, but from fury. I could feel it radiating off her.

"We can't hold it," I said. "We need to go. *Now*."

She broke free from her haze for a half second, then nodded. "The safe room."

We sprinted the last twenty yards through the gate Ember had opened earlier and headed straight into the barn. The smoke now blowing lower off the mountain and thick as soup.

Ember reached the safe room door first, but she fumbled with the latch, her hands trembling so hard she missed the lock.

"Let me," I said, gently taking the key and reaching around her side. She complied, looking back out the barn door towards the flames roaring toward us.

The lock clicked, the door creaked open, and we ducked down the stairs inside just as the world outside roared.

The safe room is small but solid; metal walls lined over concrete, surrounded by dirt and a damper vent in the wall. The door had sealed shut behind us with a metallic *thunk*, locking out the fire, but not the weight that felt like it was pressing in from every direction. This room was built to hold, but I know that the worst fire may not be the one outside.

A blue fifty-five-gallon food grade drum labeled "water" is stashed in the corner, next to a crate of supplies, a go bag, and an old Bible sitting on top of a pile of canned goods. I recognize that bible as the one that used to rest on the fireplace in the old house.

We hunker down, sitting shoulder to shoulder on the concrete bench. My hand resting on my Pulaski. Embers chest is heaving, her chin tilted back so her head rests on the wall.

Outside, the fire is running on the ridge. The vibrations from trees falling and what can only be described as the sound of a freight train, rumble through the ground. The low whine of hot wind whistling close echoes through the vent. Sweat rolls down my back, but I don't shift.

I close my eyes for just a second and start to pray again, like I always do when the fire is close. My words come out quiet and steady. I ask for strength, for wisdom, for calm in the middle of the storm. And above all, I pray for her, and for the ability to keep Ember safe.

Ember stands and moves away from me when she hears my prayer.

"You okay?" I ask her when I'm done.

"Just don't care to hear you pray." She's crossed her arms over her chest and taken a defensive posture like the words hurt her physically.

I don't say anything out loud at first. I know that this woman has been through hell, but I am also surprised. Ember was always in church leading the youth, praying for anyone that needed it, worshiping like Jesus was right in front of her. Now, the callus on her heart has taken that from her. "I'm sorry to hear you say that."

"Say what? That I don't want to hear you pray?" She throws her hands up as she continues talking, "How can a God that I have loved since I was small, that my family was devoted to, take so much from me? All of them, Rex! He took all of them!" Her chest is heaving as her emotions escalate. Her eyes full of anger and sadness, but at least she's talking. "I wasn't even hear for them! I was having a wonderful time in the middle of an ocean, thinking about nothing but myself, and Katie, and…"

She stops suddenly, like the reserve air she had just left her tank. Her arms drop to her sides as she lets her body breathe in and out, her eyes closed now. She looks like she's counting breaths in her head, in and out.

I stand and close the already narrow distance between us. "Tell me, Em. What is it that just stole the breath from your lungs? What were you going to say?"

I reach my hands up to her arms, just above her elbows and gently rub my thumbs over the inside of her bicep attempting to be a calming motion. Her body is shaking as she continues to breathe slowly. Her eyes are still closed, but I can tell she's fighting back tears when she tips her head back to try to keep them from falling. Her eyes betray her, and the first tear falls down her right cheek, leaving a trail through the ash on her face.

I lift my hand to wipe it away with my pointer finger. As my skin touches hers, her eyes open. Those blue topaz eyes shining brighter than normal through the salty tears hanging there. The color of her eyes are like the shallow parts of the ocean over sand, turquoise and vibrant. When I wipe her tear away, I wrap it into my palm. As if locking it away in my hand will keep it from falling further.

"This wasn't supposed to happen again." Her voice cracked on the word *again*.

I swallowed the lump in my throat. "I know."

"No, you don't," she snapped. Her eyes met mine, full of smoke and fury. "You *think* you do, but you don't. I rebuilt. I planned. I cleared fuel lines, reinforced this barn, and watched every wind report like my life

132

depended on it. And it still wasn't enough."

I nodded, slowly. "You did everything right."

Her laugh was sharp and ugly as she sits back down on the bench. "Then why does it feel like I'm back on that cruise, Rex? Watching my whole life disappear from a distance."

That hit hard.

I moved to sit beside her, my shoulder barely touching hers. The heat from her skin was electric.

"I remember that night too," I said quietly. "I've never forgotten it."

She looked at me sideways. "Yeah? Do you remember the way I stood there smiling? Waiting for you? While you were trying to hide from me that my family was dead?"

The words cut deep, but I didn't flinch.

"I remember the exact second I saw you on those stairs. I remember thinking something had broken inside you—and praying that it wasn't something that had to do with me." She shook her head, like shame is washing over her anew. "And then you said we needed to call home, and Chief Warren told me they were gone. That they didn't make it out. That a wall of flame swallowed the ranch and there was nothing left."

A silence dropped between us like a weight.

She pulled her knees to her chest. "You know what I hate the most?" she whispered.

I waited quietly for her next words.

"That I wasn't here. That I was off smiling, dancing, and laughing. With you."

"Em..." My voice broke at her last words.

"No. Let me say it." She looked up, tears streaming down her cheeks again. "I wanted to believe that wasn't the last time I'd laugh like that. That God wouldn't let that kind of pain happen again. But then today, seeing the fire coming at the ranch, I can't help but feel..." She pressed her palms to her eyes. "Why does He let it happen, Rex? Why does He take everything and leave me with nothing but guilt and smoke?"

I drew a breath, slow and shallow. "I don't know."

Her head jerked up.

"I don't," I said again, quieter. "I've

asked Him that same question a hundred times. When I fell to my knees on that cruise deck, when I walked into the church with you for their funeral, when I watched you fall apart every single day and couldn't do a thing to stop it or help you. The only thing I could do was pray."

She blinked at me. Her lips trembled. Even in her grief and pain, covered in ash, and her hair windblown, she is beautiful.

"I don't know why God didn't stop the fire. I don't know why you weren't there, or why they were. But I know this..." I paused, my voice low and shaking. "He never left *you*."

The sound of our hearts beating is suddenly deafening in the small space. Then another moment passes.

She stared at me like I'd grown a second head before the sound of her voice, full of ire, spoke low, "You're serious?"

"I am."

She stands to her feet again. Pacing now, her boots echoing in the room. "You think God stayed with me when He let my family die? When He let me come home to nothing but ash?"

"I think God knew what would happen and did what he could to have people who care about you near you. And He put people in your life to remind you of that."

She looked down at me, eyes blazing. "Like who? *You*?"

It's accusatory, but I own it. I stood slowly and moved toward her, just within arm's reach. "Yeah. Maybe me."

That broke her. Embers palms land flat on my chest as she shoved me once. Not hard, but not soft, either. I absorb it.

"You think I wanted *you* to be the one to hold me while my world shattered?" Her voice shook. "You think I don't relive that night on the ship every single time I smell smoke?"

"I relive it too," I said, not moving. "Every time I jump into a fire, I see your face. I hear you scream. I see you collapse, and I hate that I couldn't stop it."

She stepped back, turned away, and covered her face.

"I'm tired, Rex." Her voice is so low, I am not sure I heard her.

"I know," I take another step closer to

her.

"Tired of being the girl who lost everything."

"You're not the girl who lost everything. You're the woman who stayed. The one who rebuilt. The amazing woman who cut line, dropped fence, trusted her dog, and released her stubborn horse. You're the strongest person I know, Ember."

She let out a laugh that was wet and bitter. "I don't feel strong."

"You don't have to feel it for it to be true."

She sank down to the floor. I sat beside her, and she leaned into my side. For a while, we just sat.

Outside, the fire cracked and raged. The safe room shook with wind and pressure.

Inside, we just breathed. Then I feel her head rest on my shoulder.

"You're not supposed to be here," it barely comes out as a whisper from her lips. She looks away from me then, but she hasn't pulled away from me either. "No one else is supposed to get hurt."

"I was coming here even before I knew you were on the ranch. Chief radioed in that you were back, and refusing evac, moments before I stepped out of the back of the plane," she looks up at me for a moment and I try to muster a small grin in her direction as our eyes lock, "but if I had known you were here on the ranch, I would've come a long time ago."

I see her head lift for a moment as she turns to look at me, straight on. Her eyes are full of unshed tears, but I hear her breathing slow. Minutes pass, like she is processing internally; I hold her gaze and bring my hand to her cheek, gently touching her. At some point, her head dropped back to my shoulder. I didn't move. Didn't dare. Not because I thought she'd break, but because I wasn't sure that I wouldn't.

I'd jumped into fires all over the west. California. Idaho. Arizona. I'd cut line through forests and valleys that looked more like battlefields than land. I'd dropped into hell at night and climbed out before sunrise.

But nothing had ever felt like this.

Not because of the flames, but because of Ember. The undying smolder of what I never had the courage to go after before the fire, but what I also never let go of after. The kernels of emotion tied to her.

I knew that no matter what I did, no matter how fast I ran, how hard I fought, I would never be able to undo what she'd lost. And I couldn't fix it either.

But I could stand in it with her.

"I didn't want anyone to know I was here. It's better that way." She's looking at the floor now.

"Ember, why do you think that?" It's a genuine question.

Her body releases a haggard breath, "If no one knows I am here, then no one can pass judgment. Or pity."

It hits me in the moment the guilt she's been carrying all these years. She blames herself for not being here and thinks others blame her for not being here too.

"My sweet Em," I shift my body so that I can put my finger under chin and lift her face to look up, meeting her eyes, "No one blames you. You couldn't have done anything to save your family, and if you would've been here, you would be dead too."

"You don't know that." she whispers. "Maybe I could've made a difference."

"There were 11 people here, Em. 11 people who would be glad to know you lived. 11 people who would want to see you go on. 11 people who wouldn't want you to turn your back on God because they're gone. 11 people who you might not have gotten to say goodbye to, but they loved you so much. And I know they will all be waiting at the gates of Heaven for you when it's your time. Your life has a purpose Em, and God has you here on this Earth right now for a reason. Even if you can't see it yet."

Tears are once again pouring down her face, sobbing at the truths I am speaking over her. Her shaking is stronger now, and her breaths are more like gasps between her sobs.

"I'm going to pull you close to me. Pull away if you want, but I think you've been alone longer than you should have been."

I expect her to pull away, but instead she melts into me when I draw her close. The sobbing becomes more audible, filling the small space. I have a feeling she has been holding on to those feelings, and holding back her tears, all these years.

"Shhh…" I continue holding Ember close with one arm while I run my hand over her hair, tracing the hair from the top of her head, past her ear, and then repeat it again and again. "Ember it's okay to feel all the feelings you do. I'm here, let it all out."

"What if there's never a safe place again?" she asks.

I reached down, my hand brushing hers. "There won't be," I said honestly. "Not here. Not in this world. Not on this side of Heaven."

She blinked, looking at me confused.

"But there's still peace. And there's still hope. Even in the middle of the fire."

"And if I don't feel it?" Her lip trembled but I didn't pull away.

"Do you remember when Elijah was so tired, and God let him lay down and sleep, then woke him to eat before he slept again?" I feel her head nod slightly against my chest. "Em, I don't think you have really rested or recovered since your family died. Perhaps you need to rest in Him. Even if you don't feel it, God will carry you when you don't feel you can. And if you let me, I will help too."

As if my words trigger something inside of her, she relaxes in my arms while she continues to cry. I scoop her up from the floor and cradle her in my lap before I sit down on the bench. I keep one arm around her shoulder and let her feet rest next to me while I stroke her hair.

We sit like that for a long time. Ember sobbing. Me holding her. And she may not want to hear it, but I pray over her. *"God, Embers been through so much. She hurts tremendously, and I think she has felt guilt and loneliness for a long time. I know she loves you and doesn't understand the reason why things have happened in her life. But God, I pray that you would bring her peace and healing and show her that you can make beauty from ashes. You, Lord, bring peace to your people. Lord, if this is where I am supposed to be, for her, show me that too. I have always cared about her. I want to see her made whole. Thank you, Lord. Amen."*

When I'm done praying, I start humming a worship song, a tune I once heard on a California mountains side. I continue holding her in my arms as she softly cries.

I don't know how much time has passed, but I realize that Ember's breathing has regulated, and she has drifted off to sleep. For the first time since I laid eyes on her earlier today, she looks peaceful. I don't want to move and wake her, so instead I lean my head back against the wall and close my eyes. I have slept in worse places in more uncomfortable positions.

Sitting here holding her, I realize how physically sturdy and yet simultaneously emotionally frail she is. Her skin is golden from the time she spends outside tending to the ranch, her freckles like stars across her face. I can't help but wonder what this woman has been doing the last few years and how alone she must've felt.

I'm here now. I found her. I'm not leaving anytime soon.

Chapter 15
Quiet Outside

EMBER

I wake up in Rex's arms, and I am slightly embarrassed. I slowly move from his lap to standing, before pulling out the fold out cot Jackson put in here.

I pop the cot out, then sit down and run my fingers through my windblown hair. I open bottled water from my go bag, a granola bar, and sat quietly, letting Rex rest.

Watching him sleep it hits me how he has always been there, even when I pushed him away. He said he prayed for me, and he would have come sooner if he would've known I was here. And knowing Rex, I know that is truth; he is a man of his word.

I stand up and retrieve my family bible and flip to the verse he used during his prayer. It's one I know well, one of my favorite Christian songs recites the lyrics, and Momma used to sing it while cooking. The binding creaks open on the bible, and the frail pages whisper as they turn until I reach it, Isaiah 61:3 - *and provide for those who grieve in Zion – to bestow on them a crown of beauty instead of ashes, the oil of joy instead of mourning, and a garment of praise instead of a spirit of despair. They will be called oaks of righteousness, a planting of the Lord for the display of his splendor.*

I am not whole, not anywhere near it. But I want to be. Maybe we are in this room together for a reason. I say a little prayer to God, just in my head, I am not ready to say it out loud yet. *God, hi… I am not sure what to say, but I am here. I am trying.*

It's not much, but it's a start.

"Hi." Rex says a while later.

"Hi." I say quietly, the Bible still open in my lap.

"How are you?" he asks.

I shrug before I loop the rubber band around my freshly braided hair and toss the braid over my shoulder. It's a useless movement, really, one I've done a thousand times when I don't know what else to do with my hands. But when I glance up, he's looking at me like it's the first time he's ever seen me.

Not the girl from the ranch. Not the one who ran off to school. Just me. Here. Ash-streaked, exhausted, alive.

"You always do that," Rex says softly with a small grin.

"Do what?"

"Toss your braid like that. Usually when

you're pretending you're fine."

The words settle in my chest like warmth instead of weight. I don't know how he remembers something so small. Or maybe I do. Because I remember things about him too: the way he always checked for his lucky toothpick in the band of his hat before heading out to ride, the way he would wear socks with flipflops when he cleaned his boots, like he couldn't take his socks off, and the way he would separate out his vegetables on the plate and eat them one at a time — even in his twenties on that cruise.

I meet his eyes, and for the first time in what feels like hours, neither of us looks away.

"I really thought I could handle this," I whisper. "All of it. Alone."

His expression softens, but he doesn't say *I told you so*. He just shifts closer, sitting across from me now, and lets the silence hold the truth we both know.

"You did handle it," he says after a moment. "You still are."

My throat tightens, and I don't trust my

voice enough to answer. So, I don't. I just let myself look at him, really and truly look at him. In that quiet stillness, I remember why I let myself care in the first place. Why deep down, I never stopped.

Rex reaches over, not fast, or forceful, just steady, and brushes a smudge of ash from my cheek with his thumb. His fingers linger, and for one second, the fear, the fire, the grief — they all go quiet.

Just like outside.

"The fires passed now. It sounds quiet outside," he says it so softly, like he's afraid of disturbing this moment. I nod. "Ready to open the door?"

"Yes. Let's see what's left." I say tentatively. The silence stretched out long and tense.

Not just the silence in the air — but the kind of silence that settled between two people when they'd come through something bigger than themselves. Something consuming, that left deep scars.

Rex shifted beside me, then slowly stood and moved toward the safe room door. The metal still radiated warmth but not like before; the fire had truly passed.

He hesitated, one hand on the latch. Then he looked back at me and held out his hand.

My heart did something strange and sudden in my chest. It wasn't the panicked pounding from earlier. It was something steady, like the beating finally found the right rhythm.

I reached toward Rex's hand. His fingers are warm, steady, and real. I didn't realize how badly I'd needed to feel something *real* until that moment.

He pushed open the door and takes the first few steps.

We had been in that safe room longer than I'd liked, but opening the door felt like a portion of the heaviness had gone with it. Like a purge of the land also took pieces of the grief that I had still held. And Rex? Rex had been there with me, hearing me, holding me, and waiting for me.

The air rushing down the stairs still tastes like ash, but the sky outside has some blue to it now. The wind had pushed the smoke away from us, at least for the moment.

Rex leads me up the final steps. I don't let go of his hand, and he doesn't let go of mine either.

The fire had come down the mountainside and fueled by the tall grass, ran straight to the shed. The shed was gone now, just remnants of a building left where it once stood; the hay inside further fueled the fires consumption. Thankfully, the house and the barn still stood, the burn pattern followed around the edges of the water we had spilled out moments before we took refuge in the shelter. For the most part, the barn and house are just a little singed, but they're standing.

The fire is still too close for comfort, but we are out of immediate harm for now. To the west is an area that the fire missed, just beyond the creek. If the fire jumps it, we will be right back in the fire's path.

"Command to Smoke. Do you copy?"

The crackle of the radio surprises me and I jump. Rex reaches for his radio to respond.

"Copy Command. Go ahead."

"What's your status?"

"Most of the green zone is black zone now, but civilian Ember Greene's been located. She's with me. The fires moved past us." He looks at me as he says it. He looks relieved to say the words, and in my heart, I am relieved Rex is here too.

"Evac status, Smoke?"

I crinkle my nose inquisitively at the continued reference to Smoke. What is that about?

"Negative command. Roads still blocked with a disabled vehicle and trailer on it. Fire is to the east of us. West is clear but if the wind shifts we would have no cover to leave on foot."

"Understood. Hold your position and we will update with evac options."

"Copy. Smoke out."

I cross my arms over my chest and look at him. I am not sure whether to laugh or not, but I can't help but keep a small smile from creeping across my face.

"Smoke," he points to his shirt as he says it, pointing at the name on his shirt that I had all but missed until now. "I, uh, might have filled the firehouse with smoke my first week at the station. Managed to toss a pot mitt on a still hot stove and it caught fire and filled the place with smoke. Started as a funny jab, then it stuck."

REX

Ember stares at me for a moment, her blue eyes shining in the sunlight that has broken through the smoke. Her mouth starts to turn up, and then she starts laughing — her mouth opens wide, head thrown back, knee-slapping laughter. I'm not sure what's so funny, but she's losing her mind with laughter.

"Why are you laughing?" I ask, rather seriously.

She shakes her head, tears streaming down her face as her laughter continues. Finally, she wipes her cheeks and manages to speak through the gasps for air.

"You joined the fire department as a smokejumper, then filled the station with smoke your first week? The irony is too perfect!"

"I didn't *set* the firehouse on fire," I protest. "Just filled it with a little smoke. We had a call, I left in a rush, and I didn't realize the stove was still hot."

She dissolves into another fit of laughter, and despite being the butt of the joke, I can't help but laugh along. The sound of her laugh is beautiful, pure, and for a moment, we are just two people standing in the aftermath, finding light.

"You're right," I admit. "Smoke and Ember. Who would've thought?" Then I start laughing.

We laugh together, and I could do this every day — laugh, smile, and just breathe.

With Ember.

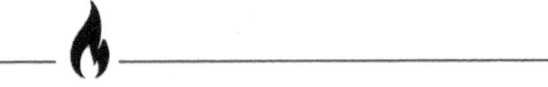

The world is black and gray now. My boots crunch over charred earth as I walk the edge of the pasture, eyes scanning for hot spots. The scorched ground radiates heat beneath my soles, and the air tastes of ash and pine resin.

I glance back at Ember, moving steadily behind me. There's grit in her step, even when exhaustion clings to her frame. Every step feels heavy, but we keep moving.

She takes note of the damages — sheds lost, the sheep's winter shelter is gone, fence posts are burned halfway around the ranch, and panes of glass busted in the barn windows from the heat. I'm working alongside her, shovel in hand, smothering the occasional smoldering patch. The main fire line held; the barn and house are mostly unscathed minus some singing.

We circle back toward the barn together, quiet but not tense. There's a new kind of peace now. The fire seems to have burned off more than just dry brush. It seems to have also burned through some of the barriers between the two of us.

Inside the barn, I lean against a cool beam, staring out at the blue and grey swirled sky. Ember walks in and hands me a bottle of water. I take a drink and let it wash away the dryness in my throat, "Why did you come back?" I ask.

She hesitates. "I'm not sure I want to say it out loud."

"Tell me," I say, turning toward her. "Please."

She looks away for a moment, then back again. "I never planned to come back. I leased the grazing land to Mr. Cooper for years so that it was maintained at least. I went to vet school, graduated top of my class. I took a job in Arizona. Then one day, this dog was brought in, burned and scared. The smell, the sight... I couldn't handle it. It made me think of them, what they went through, the smell of the bodies, the ravaging of the land. I packed a bag that night and drove here."

"Ember..."

"Don't be sorry. I chose it. I chose to come back. I chose everything."

"How long have you been back?" I take a small step toward her as I ask.

"A year. Katie and her family know I am here. Her dad built some glamping cabins nearby and checks in now and then. Her mom hosts an author writing retreat there once a year. That's how I get what I need, they help me out a lot. I haven't been to town since I came home."

"Not once?" I ask surprised, but not

shocked. No one has seen her, and in a small town, everyone would have known.

"It doesn't feel right," she says. "This place... It's still every one of them. It's quiet without them, but it's also loud with memories. I don't know how to be here without all of it."

I nod, swallowing hard. "But you're here. You're trying."

"I designed the safe room myself, with a little help from Jackson," she says, voice quiet. "Learned to clear brush, fight small wildland fires, and care for the land to avoid fires where I can. No one was going to save me again. I had to do it myself."

"You did good, Em."

She shrugs. "Doesn't feel like it."

"It does to me. You put a lot of hard work in."

A silence fills the air. The two of us trying to identify what this is now. Who we are after the fire.

She breaks the silence when she turns to face me, "Why are you here, Rex?"

"I jumped in."

"No, why are you *here*, in Montana?"

"That," I let out a breath. "Momma got sick, so I came back to help. Was only supposed to be temporary, but then she passed. I stayed."

She softens. "I'm so sorry, Rex. I didn't know."

"She's with Jesus now. Fully healed. I can handle that, even on the days that I want to pick up the phone and call her."

She's quiet for a moment, "I want to believe that. I still love God, but I'm also still mad. I lost *everything* in that fire. Where was He?" Her question comes out less angry this time, and more like a plea.

"I don't have every answer," I say gently. "But He is still good, and He does good things. Like putting me on that cruise, right before it happened."

"You think that was God?"

"I do." I walk to the open barn door and lean my shoulder into the frame as I watch the fire burn in the distance, still moving away from us. "I got a call two nights before the cruise. My old Sargent Major and his wife had booked the cruise and suddenly weren't able to go. He knew that I was waiting on starting smoke jumper school in a few weeks and had some time on my hands. I told him no originally, but that next morning as I was praying, I heard God tell me to go on that cruise. No questions in my mind it was his voice.

"I called my Sargeant Major back, and the tickets were still available, so I took them. Flew into Miami just in time to get on that ship. Spent a few days just walking, talking, and praying. I thought I was there to spend time with God, then I ran into you." I turn to her then and reach for her hand. She doesn't immediately reach back, but after a moment she steps toward me and slides her hand into mine. "Ember, I think God put me there for you."

Her voice cracks. "Do you think my family would be mad at me for staying away so long? For not even wanting to be here?"

"No," I whisper. "They'd understand. Your parents were some of the most understanding people I have ever known, and I believe that if they knew how much pain this land holds for you, they would tell you to go."

She leans into me, her head resting against my chest. I wrap my arms around her and run my hand down her braid.

"You don't have to stay here if you don't

want to," I speak softly to her. "You can go anywhere. I'll take you away if you need to go, even if it is just for a while."

She doesn't answer out loud, but I feel her nod.

I feel her shoulders shake, and I realize she is crying again. But then I hear her laughing softly, "Tommy would be so mad I'm hugging you."

I huff a laugh too, "Tommy would definitely take me behind the barn for a harsh scolding for being this close to you." I run her braid through my hand again; her hair is so soft.

She looks up at me then, a small but real smile on her face. "That night on the ship...," she takes a breath, then starts again. "I was thinking about you. About all the feelings I had for you."

My heart lurches. "Em, I had been praying about my feelings for you and how to tell you just before the call came in."

"But afterwards, I felt so guilty for being happy," she says. "For dreaming about you, and what an *us* could look like, while they were here, dying."

"You are not alone in that, Em. I carry

that guilt too. But I believe the God who holds our future still has good planned."

She wipes her face. "I'm broken, Rex."

"I'll walk with you while you heal, Em. I will pray with you, and for you, and for us, if you will let me. Drought, fire, blizzard, flood, you name it. I want to be with you, even after all this time."

"Rex," she whispers, "you still want to be with me?"

"Yes, Ember. My feelings have never changed. I have always cared for you, and always will, no matter what comes next."

She looks up at me for a moment, tilting her head, reading me. I smile at her, and then she smiles back. "Good. I have always had feelings for you too, even when I pushed you away."

I nod, an understanding passing between us. We both had been hurt then, but now we were making headway on what comes next. But there is something I don't want to wait for any longer.

"Em... there was something I really wanted to ask you on that cruise. I hope it's not too soon to ask now," I pause, waiting to see her reaction. She gives a slight nod, and I ask, "Ember Lynn Greene, may I kiss you?"

Her blue eyes close for a moment, before they open with a joy I haven't seen since we were on that ship. Then a whisper, "Yes."

I wait. A breath. Two. Before I move in to kiss her, I take in all her beauty. Even here in the barn, covered in ash, the smoke and fire still in the distance, she is beautiful, and this moment is perfect for what it means.

I gently cup her face between my hands then lean down to her. The kiss is gentle, sweet, and reverent-- like the prayer I prayed that night on the ship. Ember leans in, her hand holding onto my shirt, grounding herself.

It's not fireworks or cinematic chaos. It's something stronger than that. In the hush after the blaze, we bloomed together like fire followers. Where after heat and loss, sudden color appeared where the world had been ash.

I pull back slightly, reading her face. "You okay?"

She nods. "Better than okay."

I kiss her forehead. "This doesn't fix everything."

"No. But it's a start," she says as she smiles.

And it was.

Chapter 16
Beauty From Ashes

EMBER

The fire continued to move away from the ranch; the winds have kept it from moving west. Between that and a burn out we did after leaving the safe room, Rex feels like we're safe for now.

We still don't have a way out other than on foot, and the sun has already started to dip behind the ridge. The last threads of daylight are fading fast.

Rex has been reinforcing the fire line around the house and barn, patching any spots that look weak. When I hear his boots hit the porch, they sound heavier, tired. I meet him at the door with a tall glass of water.

"I made dinner. Well, my version of it at least, I know it's not your mom's cooking. And I wasn't expecting a guest, so I didn't have anything thawed. But... I did have all the stuff for a PBJB," I say with a grin, hoping he remembers.

The smile on his face, the one that pulls up to his ears and deepens his dimples, tells me he does. "I haven't had one of those in years. That sounds like a five-star dinner if I ever had one."

"Good. Wash your hands and meet me in the kitchen." I smile as I point down the hall where the powder room is.

A few minutes later, Rex returns with clean hands and a washed face. He's ruggedly handsome. He always has been, but now, the steadiness in his eyes draws me in even more. From the time I was little, I always thought there was something special about him. But he was Tommy's best friend, so he was always off-limits.

For the first time in a long time, I smile at a memory, instead of cry. The memory of Tommy reading my diary out loud, something about how cute Rex looked after a cattle drive; Tommy had teased me for weeks. While I don't cry, it does tug my heart. I really miss him.

I bring over a plate with the PBJB already made, and a little pile of chocolate candies on the side — another throwback to our youth. Ms. Sally had always given us kids chocolate chips on our plates as a treat.

"Peanut butter, jelly, banana... and chocolate. Every fireman's dream dinner," he says, grinning.

REX

Dinner is simple and quiet. The air around us doesn't need to be filled, it feels full and peaceful. Ember keeps glancing at me like she's trying to say something but isn't quite ready. I let her take her time.

When the last bite is gone and the dishes are rinsed, we step out onto the front porch. The sun is gone but the sky is still streaked with orange and purple fading to navy blue behind us. Smoke still hangs in the air, but it's more distant now.

Ember sinks into the swing and pulls her knees to her chest. I sit beside her, close enough that our shoulders touch.

"I don't know what happens next," she says softly. "But for the first time in a long time, I'm not scared to find out."

"Neither am I." I reach for her hand, and she doesn't hesitate to take mine.

"I think I've felt something for you for a long time," she continues, her voice low. "Even before the cruise, when we were still young. But you were Tommy's best friend. That made you off-limits. And I was younger... I didn't want you to think it was just a crush."

"I never thought that," I say, brushing my thumb over her knuckles. "I felt it too. But you were his sister. And I was older. It didn't feel fair to you, or to him. So, I told myself I couldn't go there. Didn't mean I didn't want to."

She turns toward me, our hands still joined. "I'm glad we waited. Even if the wait hurt."

"Me too."

We sit in the silence, letting it settle between us. The breeze tugs at her hair, and the last pink streaks of sunset fade behind the mountains.

"I am sorry I pushed you away, Rex. I didn't know how to feel, or how to respond," she says. "I said yes to dinner on the ship, but only to dinner. There were lines I wasn't willing to cross. Then you were there all the time, and I was worried in my grief that I couldn't trust myself."

"I know," I say. "That's one of the things I've always admired about you. You draw hard lines, and keep them."

Her smile is slow but real. "I think we were waiting for the right time. And maybe... this is it."

I reach up, brushing a loose strand of red hair from her cheek. "I think this could be it. The start of something beautiful. Beauty from ashes."

Her eyes don't waver. "Momma and Grandma always liked that verse."

"I believe in that, Ember."

"If this is the beginning of that, then I do too."

Six years ago, the fire was never supposed to be the ending of a book, it was just a chapter. Now, we are starting a new chapter together. One I believe that we were always meant to write.

EMBER

My heart is still catching up to what has happened today. Rex showing up, the fire, the kiss. Finally, after all these years. But it wasn't just the kiss. It was all of it. The honesty. The respect. The timing. The way he's never given up on me. I truly believe that we could have rushed this years ago, but it wouldn't have been right. Now? Now it feels real, safe, and worth the wait.

We sit for a long time, fingers entwined, letting the quiet settle around us like a warm blanket. The porch swing creaks beneath us. The ranch feels different now, like it is somehow rooted. That's what this is, starting over. Together.

The silence isn't empty tonight. It's full of hope, for something that is beginning. I rest my head on Rex's shoulder, and he leans into me, steady and sure.

For the first time in forever, I feel like home isn't just a place, it's a person too.

Out in the field, I hear hooves. I stand and move toward the field. There, through the shadows, I see them.

"The animals," I whisper. "They came back."

Rex steps up beside me, "Yeah. Look at that. Buck leads the charge."

We watch together as the ramshackle herd trickles in — dust-covered and ash-flecked, but alive.

"They knew where home was," he says.

I nod, eyes burning with fresh tears. "They always do."

REX

The next few days blur in a rhythm of repair and recovery. Rescue team couldn't get to us that first night, so I slept in the guest room. I left the next day when rescue showed up, but Ember stayed to tend to the animals.

I sealed my promises with a kiss and quiet words exchanged on the porch. I had to return to the station — duty always calls during fire season.

When I walked back into the fire house, I carried the scent of pine and something else with me — something Ember had left behind, just by believing again. In me, in herself, and in God.

The guys asked questions, but I only answered the ones that mattered.

Yes, I'd jumped into the fire.

Yes, I'd helped hold the line.

No, I wasn't done there yet.

I put in a forty-eight-hour shift, rotating through briefings, and half-slept nights on the truck bench. The fire moved slower now, held back by burn lines and the grace of a shift in the wind. On the third morning, I packed my gear and checked out early with the chief's blessing. He didn't ask questions, just nodded and said, "Some things are more important than smoke."

I made it back to Ember's by late afternoon. She was in the field, coaxing a young ewe toward a shady patch near the barn. She looked up like she knew I was coming, like she'd been listening for the sound of my truck.

We fell into step like we'd never paused: fence repair, water lines, slow evenings with hands dirty from work and hearts steady from knowing we'd finally said what needed to be said. Each night I left her with a kiss on the porch and a promise of another day tomorrow.

Katie's text comes through late at night on the satellite phone. I hand it to Ember without reading it.

Her face brightens. "They're okay. She wants to drive out next week once we've got access, I told her to wait before coming, but she said she's bringing pastries and dry shampoo."

"Sounds like she has good priorities," I chuckle.

Ember grins, "She usually does."

Chapter 17
Fresh Starts Bloom

EMBER

It's been a week since the fire came through. The fire forced me to do a lot of things, give it to God, talk to Rex, and acknowledge a community that I had shut out.

The day after the cleanup crew came through and helped clear the downed trees and my truck and trailer from the road, several ranchers nearby all came in with loads of hay, and helping hands to rebuild the fence and shed. Lots of repairs were made, hugs were given, and tears were shed. Many of the older ranchers, and some of the young ones, shared stories about times that my parents, grandparents, brother, uncle, and others had helped them out. It was nice to hear, even if all the emotions I had buried for years, poured out of my eyes while I listened.

They each left their numbers, a list of supplies they could share, and some wives left prepared meals. There was so much food that today I was taking a selection to the fire hall in Moose Hollow.

When I left this place I swore I would never return, except to visit. Then I crawled back to the ranch under the cover of night and stayed hidden. Now here I am making a very public appearance; it feels like now is the right time. Grief was what took this away from me, not these people.

I loaded up the truck floorboard and seat with dishes of lasagna, pasties (beef and potatoes wrapped in bread), and treats. I knew that the guys at the firehouse had been putting in long hours chasing down the remnants of the Blacktail Ridge fire. There was also a fireman that I was hoping to see.

Sitting at the stop sign on the outskirts of Moose Hollow waiting for traffic to clear, I take a deep breath and say a little prayer. *God, I know we are still working things out, but please be with me today. I feel like David standing before Goliath. But I know that you empowered David, and I pray that you give me strength today to slay my own Goliath. Thank you, Lord. Amen.*

With that I pulled through the intersection and drove down Main Street. I passed the old general store that has existed here for as long as the ranch. Then there's the sweet shop that grandma says has always had the same sweet smell since she was a kid, like heated sugar is stuck in the grains of the boards on the wall. I pass City Hall, the town restaurant, and the small police station that doubles as a fire house. I suddenly hope that there is enough food here for everyone.

I park the truck and breathe one last time

before I step out, closing the door behind me. I come around the other side and load my arms up with the food and treats and head to the door of the building. Fear begins to creep up, but I know that God is with me, and Rex is in that building; I can do this.

I hear the laughter and rowdy banter inside the building before I even grab the handle of the door, and for a moment I stop in my tracks. *Ember Lynn Greene it is time to stop being afraid. You know most of these people. Buckle up, Buttercup.*

I reach for the handle, and turn it, pulling the door toward me, with the containers and trays balanced on one arm. When the door opens and I step inside, silence greets me.

REX

The silence falls quickly over the room, but as soon as I see her, I know she needs noise and not to feel like a spectacle or an outcast.

"Em!" I say as I rush to her side to help her. All the trays in her arm look like they are about to topple over. "What are you doing here?"

"I had lots of extra goodies that I am never going to be able to finish, and I know all of you have been working hard. Thought I would bring them by to share." She looks around the room. Faces she knows, faces she doesn't, and some gawkers who heard she was back, but didn't believe it.

"Ember?" I hear Josh Davids say from behind my left shoulder.

She looks at me, and I smile at her, before I lean down to whisper, "You got this. Go get 'em!" She smiles back at me hesitantly, then takes a deep breath.

"Hi, Josh," she says as she smiles at him. "How's your momma?"

"My mom is good," he steps toward her then puts his arms out to hug her. She is hesitant, but then steps forward, "Ember, it's good to see you."

A few other locals step up to say hi to Ember, completely missing the tray of food and snacks that I set down on the table nearby. I stay close to Ember so that I can support her or throw her over my shoulder and run if she gets nervous, but she doesn't. They all tell her they are glad to see her, and a few ask questions. She talks with them all, and she's honest about her feelings. Says it's been hard and that she's trying. As men who work in high stress jobs, everyone in this room understands what she means.

"So, that's Ember Greene?" Mitch says with a handful of Miss Daisy's famous brownie cookies in his hand.

I smile and nod. "Yeah. That's her."

"Didn't tell me she was so pretty. Just that she was a girl from your past."

"A girl from my past that I believe is also my future."

"Rex, I don't think I have ever heard you so much as go on a second date with a woman, and now you're thinking about futures?"

I laugh but I get what he means. "You know Mitch, I would have said the same thing if I were you I am sure. But it's Ember. I have had feelings for her for years, and I have prayed for her for years. I think God has put us back together in His own timing. And to be honest, I never told you about her because there was a point in her grief that she rejected me, and I wasn't sure where that would end."

Mitch nods. He's been doing Bible study with me since we met in the military and knows how I feel about being a man of God, treating a woman, and dating to marry. There was never anyone but Em.

"Ember Lynn Greene," Chief Warren's booming voice fills the hall. "Don't you come in here, riling up my men, fattening them up with sweet treats, and not come say hello first." He manages to make it through the group standing there and approaches Ember.

She smiles, "Hi, Chief." She leans into hug him.

"Girl, the next time I say you need to evacuate..."

"Yes sir, I will. Promise."

Chief and Ember stand there a while

talking, others lingering nearby. Mitch and I make our way over to the group.

"So, is she the reason you have been unavailable for card nights?"

"Got me there," I say as I elbow him. "Some things are more important."

EMBER

The afternoon spent with the Moose Hollow Fire Department was emotionally draining. Rex finally rescued me and walked me to my truck. Said he would be by tomorrow after his shift was over. I kissed him on the cheek before I headed home.

As I headed around the last switchback and the road opened up to the house, I see Katie's new jeep waiting. It's pink with white accents, and the vanity plate says STHRNBL, because of course it does.

She's waiting on the porch in her yoga pants, oversize shirt, and tennis shoes. "Ya know Katie, you are going to have to update that license plate to say northern belle if you keep dressing like that."

Her laughter rings out clear and bubbly, "Oh doll, it's just a look. When in Rome..." she gestures to the mountains around us before coming in for a hug.

"I have missed you friend. How about some tea?" I open the door and let us in.

Katie and I sit and catch up. Her tour with her mom and dad through Europe, the amazing Scottish man she is now chatting with online that she met in Inverness, and the dozens of historic sites she visited. As quickly as she started she is done, "But I don't want to talk anymore about me, I want to talk about you." She flips her hair over her shoulder and leans in with her chin resting on her hand.

"Well, let's see. There was a fire, Buck and Misty ran the animals out, Rex Madison jumped onto my ranch, I cried a lot, and then I went into town today, the end."

Katie's jaw is on the floor, and I can't help

but laugh at her. "Ember, honey, I am not sure where to start. But did I hear you say, Rex Madison? As in the hunky cowboy-military-firefighter from the cruise Rex Madison?"

I smile then go into the details. The good, the bad, the tears. The promises, the prayers, and the growth I felt in my heart, not just for Rex, but for life, and for God.

"That fire was like a cleansing fire, Katie. It came in, did it's work, then it left."

Katie nods in agreement, a big smile on her face, "Sugar, I am so glad. You have been through so much. Any bit of happiness you can get, take it. But I hope you will also continue to pray on it and listen for answers." She gives me that look.

"Of course I will. I won't do anything brash."

"Good. I found a bible study I want to do. Mind if I come over every Monday? I am going to stay in Montana for the fall this year, maybe even the winter."

"Why Katie Darling, are you feeling all

right?" I smile. "Won't you miss the sun?"

She smiles a devious smile at me, "I hear it's bad for your skin…. Besides, I can always call dad and go home for a few days."

We laugh and catch up the rest of the day and late into the evening. What her plans are for the next few months in Montana, where she wants to go after that. Katie had studied business with an emphasis on art. She was making friends with the various galleries around the state and region and would be attending some shows in the area. Of course, she wanted me to tag along. I agreed.

That night we pulled out jammies, a bottle of sparkling water, and lit the fireplace just because we could. We reminisced about some college days, the futures we both hoped for, and the dreams we were building.

Tonight felt different, even with Katie. Like a veil has been lifted and the lights are brighter. Something is growing, and I think it's me.

I hear Rex's truck rumble up the gravel road right after Katie leaves. I meet him at the door with a hello and a kiss.

"The guys at the fire hall were amazed by you yesterday. They talked about it all day."

"I am not sure what to think about that," I tell him with a smirk. "Is that good or bad?"

"It's good, Em. They were glad to see you, and now that the ranchers, the ranch wives, and the fire department know.... you no longer have a secret. Are you okay with that?"

"I think I have to be, Rex. I am tired of being alone. I have you, and God, and I would like some of my old life back, even if I have to make it new." Rex smiles at that.

REX

I am tired, but I help Ember get chores done around the ranch. Feed the animals, clean the stalls, check the fence line, and make sure that her heart is being taken care of too.

"Em, I found something in the woods the other day when we were cleaning up. I wanted to share it with you, if that's okay?"

"Of course," she says with a smile.

"Alright. Be right back."

I head out to my truck and reach into the truck bed and pull out a long stick. I take a deep breath before I walk back to the house and open the door. When I meet her at the table, I see the look on her face, and the tears that start to gather.

"Is that?" she takes a step toward me.

"A walking stick? Yes." I hand it to her, and she turns it over in her hands, then she sees it.

In the handle I carved her initials, E.G., then put a hole in it and strung some paracord through so she would have a handle to hang it or carry it by.

"Rex, it's perfect." she rolls it over in her hands and then stands it upright, the handle coming to her shoulder, the perfect height for her. "It reminds me of my daddy's."

I nod, tears in my own eyes now. "Yeah, when I was clearing out brush I saw it leaning

184

against a log, like someone laid it there. I thought of your dad, and I couldn't leave it behind. I hope it's okay."

"It's more than okay. Thank you, Rex." She kisses me on the cheek before going to the front door and hanging the stick on a hook. "You know what that means though, right?"

"Camping trip?" I say.

She nods her head with a huge grin, "We can put the first notch in, together."

Later that evening, under a blanket of stars, Ember and I sit on the porch swing. It's quiet, except for the crackle of cedar and the far-off call of owls. Out here, the stars don't just twinkle, they have room to blaze. Just like Ember. Her light may have dimmed, but now I see a change in her. The air has returned and allowed her to breathe, and now her light will shine again.

"You were right, that God put you where I needed you. I just couldn't see that through my grief," she says softly.

I don't ask her to explain. I just nod and pull her close.

"I never stopped praying for you," I whisper.

"I know," she says. "I am ready to walk forward with you, no matter what comes."

And it feels like a reset, for both of us.

The fire will always be out there somewhere. The work is never done.

But Ember and I are not alone anymore. Not in this. Not in anything.

And as the night wrapped around us, I realized that the fire had taken a lot, but it had also left us something new: a beautiful beginning born from the ashes.

THE END

If you liked *Smoke & Ember*, turn the page to get a preview of the next book *Finding Wren*. A Tennessee firefighter story.

Sneak Peek
Strike Team Faith Book 2
Finding Wren

MITCH

Driving up the dirt mountain road toward the Greene Family Ranch, the scars from the latest fire are still visible. The ash is gone, but blackened spires stand where evergreens once stood. Nature has a funny way of recovering — even after something as devastating as that.

Smoke jumped into the Blacktail Ridge fire without me, headed to a place the Chief knew Smoke would be able to climb blind. I thought it was reckless then, but after Rex gave me Ember's story, I understood it.

It's been three months since that fire, and in those three months he went from gung-ho smokejumper to rancher cowboy. It makes sense really; as long as I have known Smoke all he talked about was growing up in Montana. Shortly after he moved here from Cali, I came too.

Leaving Cali wasn't hard, but leaving my brothers and sisters at the firehouse was. I had prayed about it though, and it always felt right. I never heard God say yes, but the pressing was there; so, I followed it.

Two Montana winters are enough for this southern boy, or at least that's what I am going to tell people. Truth is my sister's in a crumbling marriage, and my dad just passed away, so momma is gonna need me. Tennessee is calling, and it is time for me to go.

Helping Smoke pack his things in the last few days has helped me think about my own path. He asked if I wanted to talk about whatever was on my mind, I told him no then, but now I am ready to talk.

The bend in the road takes a hard right and I see the ranch open up before me. The side of the mountain where the creek runs through it is green, the other side is still black. With winter coming there won't be green here again until at least next year. The funny thing about fire though is that after a deep burn, what grows back is often richer than what was there before. Kind of like Smoke and Ember. God is doing something great with them.

Standing there last weekend watching them take vows in her home was beautiful. Someone said it was fast, but they have known each other most of their lives. Talking to them both, I think God got the timing right.

To my left I see Ember on her Appaloosa, Buck. Running full speed through the field toward the house. Behind her I see a whip of black hair, and I know that it is Katie coming up behind her on a beautiful paint. I am not sure who is enjoying themselves more, Ember and Katie, or the horses.

As I park, Ember turns toward the house, still full speed. Katie is not far behind her.

"Mitch!" Ember says as she slows her pace and dismounts near the house. "You're early!"

"Did I catch you newlyweds off guard?" the color in her cheeks pinks.

"Mitch, a lady never kisses and tells," she mimics her friend Katie's heavy North Carolina accent.

"Did you just mock me, sugar?" Katie asks as she dismounts next to Ember, and they tie up their horses —laughing like sisters.

"Never!" Ember says in the most mocking tone I can imagine her ever using. Katie and Ember both laugh.

The screen door opens and closes as Rex comes out wearing an apron and two sweet teas in his hands, "Ah! Mitch! Thought I heard your truck. Ladies how was the ride?" he hands them the drinks.

"Amazin'!" Katie says. "There is so much beauty here that the southeast doesn't have. It's such a stark contrast to the rolling green mountains of the Smokies."

I look around and can't disagree, but I still hear Tennessee calling. In my memory a sweet southern song plays on the banjo.

"Smoke, I was hoping to catch you a bit early to chat. If you have some time." Nearby Ember giggles: she giggles every time someone call's Rex 'Smoke.'

"Yeah, of course." He unties his apron and hands it to Ember, "Mind watching the grill, Mrs. Madison?"

Ember smiles at Rex like he is the only man in the world before she leans in to grab the apron, kissing him on the cheek. "Of course not, Mr. Madison."

Katie looks at me and rolls her eyes, "Newlyweds," she says. Then her and Ember take off through the screen door, chatting like women do.

I don't waste time. "I came to ask if you would pray with me, Smoke. You've been a big part of my life, and my walk with God, and I need some help."

"I am always happy to pray for you, Mitch. Do you want to talk about it first? You came all this way."

I nod my head before I lean back against

the porch post, staring out at the mountains. "You know my dad passed a few weeks ago. Now my momma's alone, and between us, my sister's in a bad marriage. As the man of the family, I can't pretend that it's not my problem."

Rex shifts, leaning forward. "You thinking about moving back?"

"I don't know for sure. I love jumping. Always have. But..." I rub my hand over my face. "Family comes first, right?"

"It should," Rex says. "Doesn't mean it's easy."

The silence stretches, filling the valley, but it's just Rex and I. He's been to war with me: in combat zones, with the enemy, and with fire.

"I keep asking God to give me an answer, but all I get is quiet. It's not like last time, where I felt a nudge."

Rex nods, "Sometimes the quiet is the answer. Sometimes it's the space where you figure out what matters."

I exhale, and my shoulders loosen a little.

"Would you pray with me, Smoke?"

"Of course." We bow our heads right there on the porch, the Montana sky wide above us. "Lord, help my brother Mitch know what is next on his path. Give him the courage to follow where you would lead him, and not just what's good for him, or what's easy. Help him care for his family, and if it's time to move, give him peace in that. If it's time to keep jumping, give him strength for that and keep him safe in the fire. Amen."

"Amen." My breath hitches, but then I let it out slowly. When we finish, he grips my shoulder.

"No matter where life takes you, I am always here and will always pray with you."

"Thanks, man." I say.

"Ready for Bible study tonight?"

"Yep. Brought your last two boxes too." I point to the truck behind me.

"Thank you. I can't believe I left them, but glad you saw them before Davids ransacked them looking for snacks." We both laugh. "When are you thinking about leaving?"

"I don't know yet. Soon." I look up at the mountains where the snow has already started to accumulate at high elevations. "Before the first big storm I think."

Smoke laughs at that, "Well, it's Montana, *that* could be tomorrow."

"Then I better get to packing myself. One more thing, Smoke." He turns to look at me, "Back home, there's a new fire division opening. I have been offered a position as a specialized fire instructor. It will be multi-discipline: fires, search and rescue, even special ops crossover programs." Rex's eyebrows rise at that last part. "If I take it, I am going to need a right-hand man. Would you be interested?"

Rex's jaw tightened a minute before it relaxed. I know that whatever choice he made, I would support it. "I don't think I can answer that right now. Ember and I said a year to think and pray on our future. But keep me in the loop."

From inside the house Ember's called Rex's name. He squeezed my shoulder once before stepping through the door to answer.

I sat there for on the porch looking out over the valley and ridge in the distance. An autumn wind picked up, carrying the smell of ash that never seemed to leave this place. I couldn't tell if it was God's silence... or a warning.

If you liked the preview for Finding Wren, you can get it now through most book retailers.

Hi Reader!

This short book was first in a series titled "Strike Team Faith." Each book will be a standalone, but characters may occasionally cross over, as they sometimes like to do. You can find more information on my website JBWritesStories.com.

If you liked my book would you take a moment to rate it on Amazon, Goodreads, Barnes & Noble, or anywhere else you buy books?

Thanks!

JB

More Books from Jenny Beth Hall

Strike Team Faith Series

Book 1- *Smoke & Ember* *

Book 2 - *Finding Wren*

Book 3 – *Tex & Bea* **2026**

Stand Alone Books

Christmas Storm at Kentucky Lake

Too Grumpy for Cupid *

*Available in Audiobook

All titles available in Large Print

ABOUT THE AUTHOR

Jenny Beth is a mom, wife, and lifelong military dependent who has called more places "home" than she can count. She grew up riding horses, hiking, and camping in the mountains of Alaska, Colorado, Montana, and Tennessee, where big skies and big-hearted people shaped her love of small towns and storytelling. A seasoned traveler who's moved around the country, she writes clean, faith-forward romance about resilient women, steadfast men, and communities that show up when it matters. Her stories are inspired by her own faith journey and by the ordinary heroes-family, friends, and strangers-who've left fingerprints on her life. When she isn't plotting porch-swing kisses and wildfire sunsets, you can find her chasing kids, planning the next trip, or hunting down the nearest bookstore.